Out of the Blue

Books by Lauraine Snelling

Hawaiian Sunrise

A Secret Refuge

Daughter of Twin Oaks
Sisters of the Confederacy

Red River of the North

An Untamed Land
A New Day Rising
A Land to Call Home
The Reapers' Song
Tender Mercies
Blessing in Disguise

High Hurdles

Olympic Dreams
DJ's Challenge
Setting the Pace
Out of the Blue
Storm Clouds
Close Quarters
Moving Up
Letting Go
Raising the Bar
Class Act

Golden Filly Series

The Race
Eagle's Wings
Go for the Glory
Kentucky Dreamer
Call for Courage
Shadow Over San Mateo
Out of the Mist
Second Wind
Close Call
The Winner's Circle

Out of the Blue

LAURAINE SNELLING

BETHANY HOUSE PUBLISHERS
MINNEAPOLIS, MINNESOTA 55438

Cover illustration by Paul Casale

Published by Bethany House Publishers
A Ministry of Bethany Fellowship International
11400 Hampshire Avenue South
Minneapolis, Minnesota 55438
www.bethanyhouse.com

Printed in the United States of America by
Bethany Press International, Minneapolis, Minnesota 55438

Library of Congress Cataloging-in-Publication Data

Snelling, Lauraine.
Out of the Blue / Lauraine Snelling.
p. cm. — (High hurdles ; 4)
Summary: Fourteen-year-old DJ is faced with a complicated dilemma when the father she's never met suddenly wants to become part of her life.
ISBN 1-55661-508-6
[1. Fathers and daughters—Fiction. 2. Horses—Fiction. 3. Christian life—Fiction.] I. Title. II. Series: Snelling, Lauraine. High hurdles ; bk. 4.
PZ7.S677Or 1996
[Fic]—dc20

96-35652
CIP
AC

To Angie Ingalsbe,

my friend and encourager.

Someday I'll be reading *your* books

starring horses and kids.

LAURAINE SNELLING fell in love with horses by age five and never outgrew it. Her first pony, Polly, deserves a book of her own. Then there was Silver, Kit—who could easily have won the award for being the most ornery horse alive—a filly named Lisa, an asthmatic registered Quarter Horse called Rowdy, and Cimeron, who belonged to Lauraine's daughter, Marie. It is Cimeron who stars in *Tragedy on the Toutle,* Lauraine's first horse novel. All of the horses were characters, and all have joined the legions of horses who now live only in memory.

While there are no horses in Lauraine's life at the moment, she finds horses to hug in her research, and dreams, like many of you, of owning one or three again. Perhaps a Percheron, a Peruvian Paso, a . . . well, you get the picture.

Lauraine lives in California with husband, Wayne, basset hound Woofer, and cockatiel Bidley. Her two sons are grown and have dogs of their own; Lauraine and Wayne often dogsit for their golden retriever granddogs. Besides writing, reading is one of her favorite pastimes.

1

EVEN IN CALIFORNIA, winter can be cold and wet.

DJ Randall sneezed, tempted to wipe her nose on her sleeve. Why hadn't she thought to bring a tissue? It would be nice if she could warm her frozen hands in her pockets, but that was tough to do when your horse's reins required two hands. Of course, it helped if the hands weren't shaking.

She glanced around to see if anyone was watching and quickly swiped her sleeve under her nose.

"Gross."

"Where'd you come from?"

"I was hiding behind the posts. What do you think?" Amy Yamamoto, DJ's best friend for all of their fourteen years, reined her gelding, Josh, next to Major. Tall DJ on the rangy bay and petite Amy on her compact sorrel kept alive the Mutt and Jeff nickname the two had earned.

Amy dug a tissue out of her jacket pocket. "Here."

"You're just like my mother."

"Hey, dweeb, you need a mother. How come we're working horses in the rain instead of home making fudge or something?"

"Popcorn sounds good."

"Fudge is better. Right now anything chocolate would

be better." Amy played turtle in her collar to stop the drips from her helmet from running down her neck. "Make that *hot* chocolate."

"It's not raining now." DJ glanced up at the dark gray sky hanging one story off the ground. A fat raindrop splattered in her eye. "So I was wrong. I'm going in—got more horses to groom."

"Lucky."

DJ signaled her Morgan-Thoroughbred, Major, to trot and circle the arena again. "Come on, fella, let's get this right so we can quit." She'd been working on rhythm to stride so that they would be more controlled in approaching jumps. She'd rather jump any day than work the flat, but today the outside jumping arena would be slippery, so flat work it was.

Flat is what DJ felt. Flat and wet. She gritted her teeth, ignored a shiver, and kept the beat of the trot. Major wanted to go to the barn as badly as she did. He snorted and picked up the pace every time they neared the gate.

"You want to stay out here all night?"

Major shook his head, and the droplets that had gathered on his mane sprayed her face.

DJ tightened the reins to bring him to a stop. She wrapped the reins around her wrist, dug the tissue out of her pocket, and blew her nose. Major's ears twitched at the honk, and he shifted his front feet. "Major, stand still." Her tone cut like a P.E. teacher barking orders. Major laid his ears back and twitched his tail. But he stood. They circled the ring once more, this time the beat perfect—no gaining, no slowing. Controlled.

"Why couldn't you do that fifteen minutes ago?" DJ leaned forward to open the gate. Major raised his head and nickered at the male figure just coming out of the barn door. "Oh, sure, say 'hi' to Joe and spray me. Some friend you are." While she grumbled, DJ swung the gate open, kneed Major through, and swung the gate closed again. All the while, Major kept his eyes on the approaching figure.

"How you doing, kid?" Joe Crowder, recently married to DJ's widowed grandmother, stopped in front of them and stroked the bay's nose. "How you doing, old buddy? Did I see you giving DJ a hard time? You wouldn't do that, would you?"

"Yeah, right. Sure he wouldn't." DJ leaned forward and stroked her horse's neck. Joe had sold her Major when he had retired from the San Francisco mounted police, taking his horse with him.

Joe rubbed Major's ears, then down the white blaze. "He never did care much for rain all those years on the force. Can't say I blame him." Joe turned and walked beside them back to the barn. "You and Amy want a ride home?"

"Do dogs bark?"

"A simple yes would be fine." His smile crinkled the skin around his blue eyes. "You look like a drowned rat."

"Gee, thanks." DJ kicked her feet from the stirrups and dropped to the ground. "Ouch."

"Cold, huh?"

"Y-e-s." She caught her upper lip between her teeth. With the easy motions of long habit, she ran the stirrups up, unbuckled the girth, and swung flat saddle and pad off in one smooth swoop. Then, grabbing a grooming bucket, she led Major out to his stall in the covered but open pens. Joe's sorrel Quarter Horse, Rambling Ranger, nickered a greeting, as did Josh.

"Get a move on," Amy said from Josh's stall. "We're supposed to be home by dark, remember?"

"Joe's giving us a ride." DJ slipped the bridle off and fixed the blue web halter in place. "Thanks, GJ." She nodded toward the filled hay sling and the measured grain in the feed bucket.

"Any time, kid." Joe picked up a brush and began grooming Major's other side. "Your mother getting home tonight, or are you coming to our house?" DJ's mother, Lindy, sold bulletproof vests, Glock guns, and other supplies to law-enforcement agencies around northern California. When she wasn't doing that, she was working on getting her master's degree. Lately, though, much of her time went to Robert, Joe's son—and DJ's soon-to-be stepfather. The thought of having a father around seemed strange to DJ because she'd never met her birth father, didn't know who he was, and didn't care to. After the wedding, she'd have brothers, too—five-year-old twin dynamos named Bobby and Billy. She had yet to tell them apart.

"Mom said she'd be home, but I never know for sure until I see her or check for messages on the machine. Sure would be nice if she had dinner ready." Only since Joe and Gran had married and Gran moved to a new home had DJ learned what it was like to be a latchkey kid. Often she cooked the evening meal for both her and her mother.

Major munched his dinner with enthusiasm, sharing some with DJ through a slobbery snort in her face.

"Ugh." DJ brushed him away. "I love you, too, but sheesh." She sneezed and clamped her brush between her knees to retrieve her tissue. "I should have brought a box full." She blew her nose again and wrinkled her face. "If I'm catching a cold, I'll—"

"Don't say that. Say, 'I'm catching a healing.'" Amy slammed her gate closed and, bucket in hand, stopped at Major's stall.

"What?"

"My mom heard a former Miss America talk about catching a healing instead of catching a cold. She said it works."

"Oh, sure. When my eyes run as fast as my nose and I

sneeze till I can't catch my breath, I'm supposed to say 'I'm catching a' . . . a what?"

"Healing, darlin'. Makes perfect sense." Joe took the brushes out of her hands and dumped them into the bucket. He slapped Major a good-night and took DJ by the arm. "Hey, it's worth a try. Of course, prayer is the first defense, but the two might work well together."

"Now you sound like Gran." DJ let him lead her out of the stall. "Night, Major." The big horse followed them and hung his head over the gate. DJ gave him a last pat before trotting off to catch up to the others. "AACHOOO!" The sneeze nearly blew her head off.

"Repeat after me, 'I am catching a healing,' " Amy chanted.

"I ab cadching a coad," DJ insisted. She wiped her eyes and breathed through her mouth. At least that part of her face worked like it should.

"Stub-born," Joe said as he joined the girls at the wide doors leading to the front of Briones Riding Academy's long, low pole barn. The rain had turned to drizzle that sparkled like falling fireworks in the glow of the mercury yard light.

"You two get your bikes, and I'll bring the truck around." Joe gave DJ's shoulders a squeeze. "Hang in there, kid, and we'll get you and your healing home."

Amy chuckled beside her. Her black hair, held back in a scrunchy like the one in DJ's wavy blond hair, glistened in the light. "You sound worse all the time."

"Thank you, Dr. Yamamoto. How am I supposed to 'catch a healing' with you telling me how yucky I sound?"

"Sorry. It slipped out. Hey, I'm just telling you what my mom said."

DJ felt like slugging her but knew it would take too much effort.

With Joe's help, they loaded the bikes into the back of

the Explorer. Both girls climbed into the front so they could share the seat and the heater on the short ride home. After dropping off Amy, they drove three houses down and into the empty drive. The kitchen window showed dark.

DJ groaned. Why couldn't her mother live up to her promises for once?

"Come on, let's go see if there's a message." Joe got out and retrieved DJ's bike from the back. He wheeled it up to the closed garage door. "Go open the door and let me in."

"All right." DJ forced herself to leave the warmth of the car and head up the walk to the front door. The wind blew right through her windbreaker and sweat shirt, knifing into her chest. The shock made her cough, which made her sneeze. By now, the tissue was too worn out to be any use. She jammed the key in the door, but it wouldn't turn. "F-fiddle. D-double fiddle." DJ sniffed, retried the key, and wished she could call her mother a few names. Why couldn't she come home like she'd said? She shoved the key at the lock again. It wouldn't even go in the slot.

"Hey, hurry up over there."

"I'm trying." DJ turned the key over. This time it slipped right in, the lock turning as smoothly as if she'd just oiled it. *Always helps if you put the key in right.* She brightened as she stepped over the threshold. Since her mother wasn't home, she could go home with Joe and Gran. That would make her feel better. She trotted across the kitchen and punched the garage door opener by the back door. The blinking red light on the answering machine caught her attention as the garage door groaned its way upward.

She punched the button on the machine. "Sorry, DJ, but I had an unexpected appointment. I know you won't mind going to Gran's. Call Joe and he will come to get you."

"No need for that, I'm right here." Joe's voice sounded loud in the stillness.

"Let me change, and I'll go home with you."

"Bring your school clothes and books, too, just in case you're spending the night."

"Right." DJ leaped up the stairs to her room and gathered her things. Amazing how much better she suddenly felt. She bounded back down to meet Joe at the front door.

"You got everything?"

"I think so." They stepped out and as DJ turned to pull the door closed, the phone rang. "Ohhh." She sighed and went back into the house.

Picking up the phone, she tried to sound as pleasant as her mother had drilled her. "Hello."

"Hello, I'd like to speak to Darla Jean Randall, please."

"Speaking." DJ cradled the phone on her shoulder. Who would be calling her? It was a man's voice after all. And he certainly didn't know enough not to call her Darla Jean. Only her mother could get away with that—and then only when she was mad.

There was a pause, then, "Darla Jean, my name is Bradley Atwood. I am your father."

2

A HORSE KICK TO THE STOMACH couldn't have shocked DJ more.

"DJ, darlin', what's wrong?" Joe put an arm around her waist.

When did Joe learn to sound so much like Gran? DJ leaned against him gratefully. She shook her head and tried to speak. *Come on, DJ, this has got to be some sort of prank.* She cleared her throat.

"Wh-who are you really? Is this some kind of twisted joke?"

"I am who I said. Bradley Atwood. Your mother and I . . . ah . . . went together when we were in high school."

"*Went* together?" The words blurted out before she could stop them.

"Well . . . I guess it was more than that." Whoever he was, he sounded uncomfortable. He sighed. "Look, Darla Jean, is your mother there?"

"My name is DJ." She wanted to shout at him, scream, slam the phone down. Instead she clipped each sound as if he were hard of hearing.

"Oh, okay . . . DJ." Now he sounded like an adult humoring a kid. He paused, waiting for an answer.

DJ's hand cramped from its death grip on the phone.

She looked up to see Joe, questions written all over his face, along with concern. He mouthed, Can I help? She shook her head.

"DJ, is Lindy there?"

"So you remember her name." The smart remark didn't help DJ to feel any better.

"Darla . . . ah . . . DJ, please."

"No, sir, she's not here. I will tell her you called, though. Please call back later." DJ set the receiver back in the cradle as if it were made of the finest eggshell. Only the focused action kept her from flinging it across the room.

"DJ, who was that? Talk to me." Joe clutched her shoulders in shaking hands.

DJ looked up into his eyes. "That was my *real* dad—or so he said."

"Oh, Lord above, be with us now," Joe breathed the prayer, then gathered her close.

DJ leaned into his strong chest. Good thing he was there, or she would be a puddle on the floor. *My dad*. Shock made her shiver.

Joe soothed her like he did the twins when one came to him with an owie. Gentle hands patted her back. "It'll be okay," he murmured. "DJ, it's going to be all right."

Suddenly she pushed herself upright. "Who does he think he is, calling like that? Just like we saw him yesterday. The jerk!" She stamped her way around the kitchen. "I don't need him. Mom doesn't need him. He didn't ever call or visit or anything. Why now? Who does he think he is anyway?" She balled her hands into hard fists and pounded the counter. Feet stamping, arms waving, she circled the room again. "I don't need a dad now." She turned to Joe. "He didn't care for fourteen years, for Pete's sake! Why now?"

"I wish I knew." Joe's voice introduced a note of calm.

DJ slammed the palms of her hands on the counter and

stayed there, elbows rigid. "Why, Joe?" She raised stark eyes to his face. "Why?" she whispered again.

"How about you let your mother deal with that? Any idea when she'll be home?"

DJ tried to remember. She *had* listened to the phone messages. *Get with the program*, she told herself.

"Take it easy, kid, you've had a pretty major shock."

"Ain't that the truth." She sucked in a deep breath and let it out. Leaning back against the counter, she absent-mindedly chewed on the cuticle of her forefinger. When she realized what she was doing, she jerked it away. "Fiddle. Double, triple, and . . . and ten times fiddle!" Her hands cried out to do something. Slamming counters hurt. So instead, she rubbed the scar in the palm of her right hand.

"Keep talking to me, darlin'."

"You say 'darlin' ' just like Gran."

"You mind?"

DJ shook her head. "I like it." She sighed again. "Guess there's nothing I can do about this, is there?"

"Pray. That's all I can do. It's the only thing that keeps me from finding out where this man lives and going there to beat the tar out of him."

Startled, DJ looked up. "You'd do that?"

"Gotta use the skills I learned at the police academy in some way." He grinned at her, then grew serious. "No, DJ, I wouldn't touch him, no matter how much I think he deserves it. But I want you to know that anyone who hurts my family has me to deal with." He jabbed a thumb at his chest.

DJ studied the big man across the kitchen. "You know what? I'm glad you're on my side."

"And I'm glad to be on your side. But let's listen to your mother's message again."

DJ shook her head. "I erased it, but I know she said she

wasn't sure when she'd be home. I guess my mind's starting to work again."

"Okay, leave her a message, then let's head for home. Melanie will be getting worried."

It still caught DJ's attention when he called Gran, Melanie. All she'd ever been to DJ was Gran. "Gran will know what to do." DJ paused. "Won't she?" On the way out the door, she wrote her mother a note and attached it to the bulletin board with a stickpin.

But Gran didn't know what to do, and when Lindy finally came to pick up her daughter, the fireworks began.

DJ watched her mother do much the same as she had—pace, yell, wave her arms. Now, sitting on the floor at her grandmother's feet with Gran's hand stroking her hair, she felt as if nothing could get to her. She leaned against her grandmother's knees and sighed.

"Do you have to call him back?"

"Not in this lifetime." Lindy clamped manicured hands on slim hips and spun around to face them. Her dark blond hair, each chin-length strand in perfect order, swung across her cheek. She hooked the curve of it over one ear, sparks flashing from her emerald eyes. The frown lines she fought so diligently deepened. "Well, Mother, what do we do now? You were the last one to talk with him."

"That was over thirteen years ago." Gran kept her hand on DJ's hair.

"I know. And I thought the agreement was that I would never ask him for support and he would never ask to see his daughter."

"It was. You both agreed to that. You were two kids who'd made some less-than-perfect choices; you each wanted to get on with your life, to move forward without any anger between you."

"I remember."

"I know you do, darlin', I just want to refresh your

memory." Gran looked to Joe, who nodded at her. "I think we got the better end of the deal by a long shot because we got Darla Jean. Brad's missed out on a lot."

"Whose side are you on, Mother?" Lindy crossed to the sofa and sank down on it, resting her elbows on her knees. She still wore a cream-colored silk suit she had dressed in for work. "You aren't saying I should call him back, are you?"

"I'm saying we need to look at the whole picture and all the people in it. We should always treat others with the respect and love with which we want to be treated. You desperately loved Brad at one time, and he loved you the same."

"I know." Lindy rubbed her temples with her fingertips. "We were so young."

DJ watched and listened as if this were the best movie ever filmed. And she was a part of it. This was her father they were talking about. Now she understood why she'd never heard about him.

"And now you're adults."

A silence, heavy with meaning, filled the room.

DJ tried to decide what she was feeling. Angry? Nope—or at least, not any longer. Scared? A bit. Curious? Big yes. She flashed a look up at Gran and received a loving one back.

I am so lucky. The thought floated into her mind and took hold. She looked up to see Joe watching her. A nod accompanied the gentle smile that barely turned up the corners of his mouth. DJ knew down deep in her heart that he wore the look of love. And it was for her.

"DJ, did you write down his number?"

DJ jerked back into the conversation and stared at her mother. *Number? Whose number?*

"Did you get Brad's number, darlin'?" Gran whispered.

DJ shrugged. "Ah . . . no. I asked him to please call back

later. Sorry, I just wasn't thinking straight."

Lindy started to say something, then just shook her head. "Guess I wouldn't be thinking too clearly in a situation like that either."

DJ looked at her mother as if she'd left a marble or two at work. *A few minutes ago, she was yelling all over the place. Now she's actually being nice. What's up?*

"That answers it, then. We wait until Brad calls back." Gran gave DJ a last pat and got to her feet. "Good thing I turned off that oven, or we'd all be eating peanut butter and jelly sandwiches for dinner." She took DJ's hand and pulled her up. "Come on, you can set the table."

After dinner, DJ and her mother drove home without saying a word. When they got to the house, Lindy checked the answering machine, but the red light lay dark. She sighed. "I'm going to call Robert. Darla Jean, I know this is hard for you. I'd give anything if Brad hadn't called, but he did, and we'll deal with it. Please don't worry about it, okay?"

DJ nodded. She kept thinking of the verse Gran had whispered in her ear as she went out the door. Gran had shared it before. It was one of those in Romans DJ had underlined. *In all things God works for the good of those who love him, who have been called according to his purpose.* She'd never quite understood the last part, but the first seemed pretty clear: God could bring good out of everything.

DJ eyed her mother, who still looked pale and upset. "Don't you worry either, Mom, okay?"

"Easier said than done," Lindy muttered. "Night, DJ. If he calls again and you answer the phone, try to get his number."

It was DJ's turn to nod. How could she have messed up like that?

When she finally snuggled under her covers to say her prayers, everything was fine—until she tried to say "amen." The word wouldn't come. She lay thinking, *God, what is it?* Often she wished He would talk to her like He had to Moses in the Old Testament. Loud and clear. But, as usual, He was silent. She sighed and flipped over. A thought trickled into her mind. *Pray for your father*.

DJ shot up so quickly, her covers flew off. "Pray for my father—you have *got* to be kidding!" She flopped back down and stared at the ceiling. Why would she do a stupid thing like that?

Why not?

She gnawed on her lip. So maybe it wasn't a big deal. She could just say "bless him" and "take care of him" and—she thought of Gran. Gran would laugh at her right now, that loving laugh that made DJ feel good.

"Godblessmyfather." It was hard to talk through gritted teeth. She sucked in a breath. "But I want to remind you, God, I really don't need another father. I'm going to have Robert, remember?" DJ bit her lip again. "Amen." Why couldn't she say that before?

She woke up crying in the middle of the night.

3

SOMEONE WAS SCREAMING.

"DJ, what is it?" Lindy entered the room in a rush. "Are you all right?"

"Huh?" DJ pulled herself out of the fog of sleep. Her throat hurt.

"You were screaming. Are you okay? What's wrong?"

DJ shook her head. "Someone was chasing me—I couldn't see who. I fell off the road and just kept falling." She clutched her aching head with both hands. Her heart felt like it would leap out of her chest. She sucked in a deep breath, but it didn't stop the pounding.

Lindy sat down on the edge of the bed. "Can I get you anything?" With one hand, she stroked DJ's shoulder.

"My head hurts." How come she felt like throwing herself into her mother's arms and bawling like a baby? DJ never did anything like that—crying was for babies.

"Let me get you some pain reliever." Lindy got up to leave, and just the movement of the bed made DJ feel like heaving. Was this what her mother's migraines felt like? How did she stand them?

But when she lay down again after her mother's ministrations, DJ felt herself drifting back into the freaky dream. It wasn't supposed to work that way. She forced her eyes open and turned on her bedside lamp. The five gold Olympic rings on the poster above her dresser gleamed in the light. *That* was the dream she lived for. Someday, she, DJ Randall, would jump in the Olympics. She would go for the gold as a member of the U.S. Equestrian Team.

DJ reached over and turned out the light again. This time, horses, horses, and more horses, all with her aboard, mastered the jumps with flying tails and happy grunts.

Rain sheeted her window when she awoke. She slapped off the alarm and sat up, leaning her head first on one shoulder, then the other. She still had the feeling that if she moved too quickly, the headache would return.

"Yuck." She hauled herself from her bed, feeling sticky and heavy. Once in the bathroom she knew why. Her pajama bottoms wore splotches of dull red. Her heart quit thundering in her ears as she realized she wasn't bleeding to death. Her first period. One more thing to deal with! She groaned. As if yesterday's events hadn't been enough.

She stared at the pale face in the mirror. Her shoulder-length blond hair hung in strings about her face. Someone had painted black circles under her green eyes, and a zit beaconed on her chin.

"I'm going back to bed." DJ fumbled under the sink for the box of pads her mother had forced on her months ago. If this was growing up, someone sure had screwed up the program. She reached to turn on the shower. If she didn't go to school, she wouldn't be going to the Academy either. That was the rule. Since DJ was almost never sick, that hadn't been a problem very often. She'd only stayed home when Gran insisted.

Instead of turning off the hot handle, she added the cold and stepped under the needle spray.

It could have been the shortest shower on record. Calling Joe for a ride to school because she'd missed the Yamamoto bus would be embarrassing. She fixed herself up, donned her one pair of black jeans, and grabbing a food bar, headed out the door on the second honk.

"Gross," Amy said with a wrinkled nose when DJ filled her in on the morning's happenings. The two sat in the second seat of the station wagon since Amy's brother, John, said the front seat was for those about to learn to drive. They didn't mind—that way, if they talked low, they could catch up on all that happened without the others hearing.

"Yeah, and that's not the half of it." DJ filled her friend in on the cataclysmic call of the night before. By the time she'd finished, they were at Acalanese High School, where they were both freshmen.

"Thanks, Dad." DJ waved as she slammed the door. Mr. Yamamoto, head of the volunteer parents for the Academy, told all the kids to call him Dad. Insisted it was easier that way.

DJ pulled her jacket over her head to keep dry and dashed after Amy. It looked like it would rain forever.

The day didn't improve much. Her history teacher finished the far from perfect morning by calling a pop quiz.

"Think I'll go eat worms," she muttered when she met Amy at their locker at lunchtime.

"Now what?"

"No lunch money."

"So share mine. I'll grab an extra salad."

"I'm starved."

"Ask if you can charge."

"I'd rather eat worms."

"Fine, be a grouch, but that's not like you."

"Maybe it's my turn." DJ dumped her books on the bottom of the locker and slung her backpack in on top. She felt like slamming the metal door and banging her fists on it. Instead she let Amy shut it and followed her friend into the lunchroom.

Thanks to Amy sharing her food, DJ's stomach quit growling. By the end of classes, she felt almost human again. Of course, the thought of Major and the Academy had nothing to do with that. Even if it was pouring, they could ride under cover.

"What are you going to do?" Amy asked as they waited outside under the overhang for Joe to arrive.

"About what?"

"Your father, silly."

"Got me. I don't have to do anything till he calls, and maybe he won't." She waved at the man driving the hunter green Explorer. "I hope he doesn't."

She answered Joe's questioning look with a shake of her head. But while it was easy to pretend to shrug the whole mess off on the outside, inside the questions raged. *What kind of man is my father? What does he do? Is he married? Do I have half brothers and sisters?*

She changed clothes in record time and hopped back into the car to go to the Academy. All the way there, the temptation to chew on her fingernails burned like a hot curling iron. To keep from giving in, she sat on her hands. *I can do all things through Christ who strengthens me. I can do all things*. Gran had given her the verse to help her overcome chewing her fingernails. They'd made a pact that if Gran could find a verse that could even apply to chewing fingernails, DJ would try to stop. So far it was working. DJ even had to file her nails once in a while.

At the Academy, she checked the white erasable duty board and saw that the outside rings were unusable—too wet. That was no surprise, the way the rain had been coming down. Since the outside work was curtailed, the academy employees had cleaned stalls and groomed the boarded horses.

"Yes!" She pumped her right arm. That meant more time to work with Major. But first she had to spend her hour working Patches, the green broke gelding she'd been training for Mrs. Johnson.

"I should put you on the hot walker," she told the fractious gelding. He rubbed his forehead against her shoulder, leaving white hairs on her black sweat shirt. "I know, you're just trying to soften me up." But she couldn't resist his pleading and gave him an extra carrot chunk from the stash she kept in the tack room refrigerator. Patches lipped the carrot from her palm, munched, and blew carrot breath in her face.

DJ attacked his heavier winter coat with brushes in both hands. By the time she had combed the tangles out of his tail and picked his hooves, she'd been over the questions in her mind for the umpteenth time. She tacked him up and led him to the wide open front door of the barn. The rain blew in sheets across the parking area.

"You sure you want to go out in that?" David Martinez, one of the older student workers, asked from the tack room. "You'll get soaked just crossing to the covered arena."

"I know." DJ led her mount to the door of the tack room. "Hand me that slicker up on the nail, would you please?"

David did as asked, shaking his head. "I skipped my workout, put my horse on the hot walker, and called it good."

"I thought about it but . . ." She finished buttoning the yellow slicker and placed her foot in the stirrup. "Okay, fella," she said, swinging into the Western saddle. "Let's do it."

Patches balked at the gate. "You sure aren't Major," DJ

muttered as she dismounted to open and close it when he finally consented to go through. Mounting into a wet saddle seat did nothing to improve her humor. "You know, Patches, if I didn't like you, I'd have left you in the barn." The gelding's ears flicked back and forth as he listened to her and checked out the arena. The rain had brought on an early dusk, so the overhead lights cast deep shadows in the corners.

DJ kept a firm grip on the reins and paid close attention to her horse. He felt like a coiled spring. She walked him around the ring, letting him get used to the arena. At last, he let out a breath and played with the bit, a sure sign he'd settled down. DJ could feel her shoulders and spine relax along with him. They settled into a jog, and for a change, Patches minded, keeping the even pace he usually fought so hard.

"What's with you today? You finally decide to be a trained mount instead of an ornery one?" Patches snorted and kept the pace. DJ nudged him into a lope, and after a few pounding steps, he settled into the rocking-chair rhythm that was such a pleasure to sit. When she pulled him back down and turned him counterclockwise, he tried to move to the center of the ring, but at DJ's insistence he went back to the rail.

So what if Brad never calls? The questions started again. DJ laid the reins over, shifted her weight, and Patches danced up the ring, changing leads like a ballroom dancer.

"DJ?"

Without warning, Patches exploded beneath her. One stiff-legged jump, as if the horse was starring in a rodeo, and DJ catapulted right over his head.

4

THOUGHT ONE: *Patches, you're dead meat.*

Thought two: *When I can breathe again, that is.* If *I can ever breathe again.*

"DJ, are you all right?" Krissie, one of her beginning students, knelt in the dirt beside her.

DJ spit out a chunk of dirt and rolled to a sitting position. One knee burned, and her chest hurt—getting the breath knocked out of you did that. Most of all, though, her pride felt like she'd landed squarely on it.

"I'll be fine." She leaned her head from side to side and sucked in a deep breath through her mouth. She gagged and choked on another chunk of dirt—at least, she hoped it was only dirt. Pulling a tissue from her pocket, she blew her nose, smearing more dirt in the process. The mess showed on the soggy tissue.

Krissie let out a wail. "It's all my fault. If I hadn't called to you . . ."

DJ shook her head. "I know better than to take my mind off Patches. He was just waiting for a chance to—that no-good, rotten hunk of horse meat. Where is he?"

"Running around the arena like he lost his mind." Krissie put a hand under DJ's arm to help her up.

Keep cool, DJ ordered herself. *How could I let that fool horse dump me? This has got to be the worst day of my life.*

DJ brushed the dirt off her jeans and turned to look for Patches. Good thing the gates had been closed, or he'd be out loose in Briones State Park or on the road by now. She gingerly took off her helmet and glanced at Krissie. Fat tears welled in her eyes, and her chin quivered.

"Hey, forget it. Remember the day you took a header?" The girl nodded. "Did you get really hurt?" Krissie shook her head. "It can happen to any rider, no matter how long you've been working with horses. You have to be careful all the time." DJ tried to keep the grumble out of her voice, but she wanted to scream and pound the fence. Or Patches.

"Go get ready for your lesson. I'll get that crazy horse."

Krissie hesitated as though she had more to say, but at DJ's frown, she trotted off.

DJ strode across the arena. When she got close, Patches threw up his head and charged past her. She tried to grab his reins but missed. Calling him every name she could think of and a few she invented, she stomped across the parking lot, the rain dripping down the neck of her slicker.

In the tack room, she found a can and scooped some grain, then rushed back across the lot to the arena, her jeans sticking to her legs. By now, Patches was having a grand time evading David.

"Patches!" DJ rattled the feed can.

The horse skidded to a halt, ears pricked. She walked toward him as he tentatively moved toward her, nose extended so he could sniff to check that she wasn't tricking him. DJ knew better than to scold him before she had a hand on his reins, so she called him names in a gentle, wheedling tone. "You stupid beast. I could brain you, you know. If I have to get someone else to help me, you are going to be very, very sorry."

Patches stopped just far enough away that she couldn't reach his reins. Good thing she'd knotted them for Mrs.

Johnson, or he'd have stepped on one and broken it. That could have hurt his mouth—and all because she wasn't paying attention. DJ shifted the name-calling to herself.

"Hey, DJ, having trouble with your horse?" Tony Andrada, his drawl proclaiming his Southern ancestry, leaned crossed arms on his horse's withers. For a while, she and Tony had really mixed it up over the rotten way he had treated her friend Hilary Jones. But lately things had been at least civil.

Except for now.

The daggers DJ shot him should have knocked him bleeding from his horse. "Why don't you go find a canyon and fall into it?"

"Whoa." Tony raised his hands and leaned backward. "S-o-r-r-y." He turned his horse away. "Just thought I could help."

DJ stood still and shook the can to rattle the grain. Patches sniffed as she dug out a handful and held it out to him. He snorted, stepped forward, lipped the grain, and reached for the can.

DJ clamped a firm hand on the reins and handed the can to David. "Here, you take this. A hammerhead like him doesn't deserve a treat." Without offering pats or soft words, she swung aboard and ordered Patches into a slow jog, the gait he hated the most. Once around the ring and she reversed, made him back up, ran through some figure eights, and headed for the gate. "Good boy." Her compliment didn't sound any friendlier than her name-calling had been.

Good thing Bridget Sommersby was gone for the day. Telling her later wouldn't be nearly as humiliating as having her watch. The owner of Briones Riding Academy had become DJ's mentor.

DJ's three girl students—Krissie, Angie, and Samantha—were riding their horses around the arena at a walk when DJ returned after putting Patches away.

DJ was in no mood to give a lesson, but since no one was asking, she gritted her teeth. On top of feeling like she'd been slugged, a case of cramps had hit in full force. Add a headache on top of that, and DJ felt like chewing nails and spitting them out machine-gun style. She rubbed her forehead. Add to the mess a new—or rather old—father, a rambunctious horse, and students who were looking at her as though she'd sprouted horns. She felt like she was trapped in the picture book Bobby and Billy, the Double Bs, loved so much—this was truly a terrible, no good, awful, very bad day. Or something like that.

She sucked in a deep breath and winced. Her ribs hurt. "Okay, kids, let's pick up the pace. Take a lesson from me and keep your concentration on what you're doing. Let's see a good ride." She watched them closely.

"Come on, Angie—back straight, relax your shoulders. Krissie, who's in control over there?" The criticisms came a little too easily. "Samantha, keep those reins even. You're confusing your horse."

By the time the lesson was over, the girls looked like whipped puppies. They quickly filed out of the gate into rain that hadn't let up an iota.

"Boy, were you hard on them or what?" Amy reined up beside DJ. She'd been circling at the far end of the arena for some time.

"Oh, knock it off. I wasn't either."

"Ex-c-u-s-e me." Amy looked closely at her friend. "You're a mess."

"Thanks a big fat lot." DJ turned and stomped through the puddles to the barn. Maybe riding Major would make her feel better. When she walked by the girls unsaddling their horses, they peeked at her out of the corners of their eyes. No playful chatter, no teasing.

DJ stopped. "Look, I get the feeling I've been a grouch.

I'm sorry. You all did fine out there."

It was as if the sun came out right there in the barn.

"Are you feeling all right?" Angie asked, always sensitive to other people's pain since she managed so much of her own.

DJ shook her head. "But that's not your problem."

"Did you get hurt hitting the ground?" Krissie's blue eyes were still troubled.

"No. Unless you call smacked pride hurt. Come on, kids, your mothers will be here soon and you need to wipe your saddles." DJ mentally added guilt to the load she was lugging around like a full feed sack.

Major greeted her with a nicker that could be heard the length of the roofed stalls. Rain drummed steadily on the corrugated fiber glass sheets overhead. Only the lights strung along the ceiling beam kept the dusk out of the stalls.

"Hi, fella. Sure glad someone is happy to see me." She dug half of a horse cookie out of her slicker pocket. "I saved this for you." She sneezed and hunted for a tissue.

Major took his treat and munched, nosing her face and shoulders at the same time. Alfalfa grain mixed with molasses smelled good to DJ, but horse smelled even better. She inhaled the horsey perfume and leaned her forehead against Major's neck. Joe had already cleaned the stall and given Major a good grooming. *If I hadn't fooled around with Patches, I would have been here doing my own work. That dumb horse. I better remind Mrs. Johnson to put him on the hot walker*. DJ sighed and rubbed her head again. If this was what migraines felt like, no wonder her mother was a bear at times.

"Come on, fella, let's get going." She snapped the lead shank on to his blue nylon halter and, unhooking the gate, led him through.

Joe met her halfway down the aisle as he returned from

working Ranger. "You okay, kid?"

"I will be."

"Heard you took a fall."

"Yeah. Later, okay?"

She could feel Joe's gaze drilling into her back as she led Major to the tack room. The girls were gone and the evening hush that came just before the adults arrived had settled on the barn. DJ put her arms around Major's neck and leaned against him. His warmth felt wonderful as it penetrated through her clothing. "What would I do without you? You big sweetie, you."

Major turned and nudged her shoulder as if to say, Come on, let's get riding. DJ hugged him again and went to get her tack. If riding Major didn't make her feel better, nothing would.

"You want to talk about it?" Joe asked on the way home.

"I'm fine." DJ dug at the snag on her cuticle.

"Sure, and I'm Madonna." Amy gave her a sour look.

"Just bug off, will ya?" The moment she said them, DJ wished she could snap the words back into her mouth. She could feel the looks Amy and Joe were swapping. No one dared to say anything more to her. Amy thanked Joe as she quickly hopped out of the truck.

"You want to come home with me?" Joe asked.

DJ shook her head. The dark house would fit the way she felt. "No, I think I'll just go to bed."

"DJ, did you get hurt out there?"

She shook her head. *How could she tell him that she felt like yuck?* She could feel the heat on her cheeks. He was a guy, for Pete's sake. She needed Gran or her mother, and neither one of them was here. She felt like bawling. How stupid!

"I'll be fine. Thanks for the ride." She bailed out and dashed up the sidewalk, waving over her shoulder. She entered the kitchen to find the red eye on the answering machine blinking.

Did she dare ignore it? Habit and her mother's drilling made her punch the button. Message one: "I'll be home later, I have a pile of paper work to clear up here." Message two: "Sorry you're not there, Darla Jean and Lindy. I will call back later." DJ recognized the voice immediately. This time, Mr. Brad Atwood gave a phone number and invited them to return his call.

"I don't need you," she growled at the phone. She punched the save button hard, as if trying to poke a hole in the machine. "You didn't need me all these years, and now I don't need you."

DJ stormed up the stairs and, after downing some ibuprofen in the bathroom, shucked her clothes and crawled into bed. Her wrist throbbed. If she never had another day like today, it would be too soon.

5

DJ'S PRIDE TURNED OUT to be the only lasting injury. Having to apologize for being a jerk the day before didn't make it better.

Amy shrugged. "Forget it. I knew you weren't your usual self. You were crazy." She sat her Western saddle down on its horn by her stall and gave Josh a pat on the nose. "See you in the ring."

"You nut!" DJ called over her shoulder. One good thing about riding English, the saddles were lighter. She opened the door to Major's stall, pushing him aside so she could squeeze in. "Hi, guy. Looks like Joe's been here." Major nuzzled her pocket. "I know, you need a treat." She dug out a carrot and stroked his forelock while he chewed. "You are so cool."

"He is, isn't he?" Joe stopped at her stall. Ranger nickered in the next box. "I'm coming, buddy."

Joe saddled the gelding and rode into the covered arena with DJ. Major pricked his ears, aware of everything around him, and settled into an easy trot that didn't even require posting. DJ could feel herself relax. Riding or even working with Major was as different from her time with Patches as birds from bumblebees.

"You've really been working with him," DJ said with a nod toward Ranger.

"Every afternoon. Except today."

"What was today?" DJ leaned forward and stroked Major's neck.

"I . . . ah—well, I checked up on Bradley Atwood."

"You what?" Major snorted at DJ's shift in position. "Easy, fella."

"I had a friend look him up in the computers, that's all. He has a clean record, owns quite a bit of land up in Santa Rosa, and has a sizable bank account."

DJ stopped Major so she could focus on what Joe was saying. "You really ran a check?"

Ranger sidestepped, wanting as always to be moving. "Yes, and your grandmother is not happy with me—or at least, that's what she claims."

"I bet. Why'd you do it?"

"Just to be safe." Joe nudged Ranger forward.

"Well, I'll be." DJ stroked Major's neck and loosened her reins. Joe was watching out for her. Major settled back into his trot, and they circled the ring. When he was warmed up, she signaled a canter. If only they were riding up in Briones. Since the rain had begun—a hundred years ago, it seemed—she and Amy hadn't ridden up in the hills.

DJ slowed the pace and rode with Amy awhile, then with Hilary. "This is like warming up before a show," DJ said with a grin.

"Yep, only without the pressure. You missing jumping as much as I do?" Hilary asked.

"Yeah, but have you looked out at that arena? Pure slop in spite of all the sand."

"I know. Maybe we could move the jumps in here. At least a couple of them."

"Bridget won't go for that."

"She did one year when it was like this. I'll ask her tomorrow. How's the dressage coming?" Hilary ran a loving hand over her horse's mane, smoothing an errant strand.

"Haven't started. Bridget's been gone and now that we're without any extra arenas, she asked if I would wait to begin. I've been working Major on the flat. He sure learns fast. Faster'n I do."

"You'll get it eventually, but it's not like jumping. Dressage takes lots and lots of drilling."

"Sounds like what I'm doing with jumping, only without ever being airborne."

Hilary's teeth showed extra white against her dark skin. "You and I like the same things. But, hey, I've got to get home. Tests tomorrow." She lifted a hand in a wave. "See ya."

"Yeah, later." DJ took Major down to the far end of the arena and began working him in a tighter circle. She might as well work him on bending. You could never do too much of that.

"See you tomorrow," Joe said when they reached her house. "I see the boys are here."

DJ groaned. "That means I'm late." She glanced at the clock on the dashboard. "Or they're early."

"Have fun."

Each twin glommed on a leg when she entered the house. DJ reached down and hugged first one, then the other.

"We was waiting for you." "Daddy said you could come help us pick out the pizza." "I want to ride." "How's Major?" The boys had a habit of talking on top of each other. Even after all these months, DJ still couldn't tell Bobby and Billy apart. Blond, curly hair topped both round faces, identical blue eyes smiled up at her, and they never stood still long enough to see if one was taller or not. To save time, DJ had nicknamed her soon-to-be brothers the Double Bs.

"Okay, guys, give DJ a chance to breathe." Robert

Crowder, a slightly taller and good deal younger version of his father, Joe, came to her rescue. "I thought maybe we would just eat out. What do you think?"

"Fine with me. Where's Mom?"

"She called from her car—should be here in a minute or two." The cellular phone in her mother's car was a gift from Robert. He said he liked knowing she was safe, especially with all the time Lindy spent on the road.

"Good, I'll change then."

"We help you." The boys took her hands. "Hurry, we's hungry."

"Nope, guys, young ladies don't need little boys to help them dress." Robert tucked a squirming body under each arm and headed for the family room. "I know there's a favorite book of yours here."

"We want Arthur and his terrible, awful . . ."

DJ shut the bedroom door on their unison voices. What would it be like after the wedding when they all lived in one house? How would she put up with them underfoot all the time?

She changed with amazing speed—her mother didn't appreciate the rich stable smells that clung to DJ after a day at the Academy. She picked up her boot and checked the bottom. Sure enough, that's what she'd been smelling. She should have known to leave her boots in the garage. Probably left bits of horse manure all through the house.

But nothing was said when Lindy arrived home, and they had a great time at the pizza parlor. DJ took the boys to watch the cooks make pizza, then fed quarters into the horse for them. She'd rather get them up on Bandit again so they could learn to ride a real horse. If only they could buy Bandit. She'd borrowed the Welsh pony several times for the little kids to ride when they had family gatherings. Robert had promised the boys ponies and dogs as soon as they moved into the house he was remodeling over by

Gran's. While it wouldn't be ready before the wedding in February, it would be soon after.

"The pizza's here." Both boys dashed back to the table. They bowed their heads and said grace before digging in.

DJ sneaked a peak at her mother. While they'd always said grace when Gran lived with them, Lindy didn't much care for it. She said she'd leave the praying to Gran—she had enough to worry about.

With one twin on either side of her, DJ didn't have time to think during the meal.

"DJ, when can we ride Major?"

"When you are bigger."

"We's bigger now. Can we ride tomorrow?"

"I don't think so." She took a bite of warm pizza and caught the thread of cheese with one finger. As she wound it around and stuck it into her mouth, she glanced at her mother. And flinched. Caught in the act. How come her mother was always looking when DJ did something silly?

Bobby and Billy both stuck their fingers in the cheese and did the same.

"Hey, guys, don't do that."

"You did."

DJ could feel her mother's withering look. And it didn't feel good.

6

"I THINK YOU SHOULD SEE YOUR FATHER," Lindy said two evenings later.

"You gotta be crazy! Why would I do that?" DJ could feel her jaw hit her chest. "You said I wouldn't have to."

"I know. I've changed my mind." Lindy sank back against the sofa as if she could no longer hold up her head. She rubbed her forehead, and the telltale gesture warned DJ that her mother was bordering on a migraine.

DJ watched her mother, hoping for a change of heart. "I talked with him on the phone. Wasn't that enough?"

"For thirty seconds?" Her mother's eyebrows lifted slightly, and she gave a minute head shake.

DJ clamped her mouth shut on all the things she wanted to say. Granted, she'd prayed for *him*, but only because the Bible said to. After all, she'd told Gran, wasn't she supposed to pray for her enemies? Gran had chuckled when DJ turned that verse on her.

But was Brad Atwood an enemy?

"So, will you?"

"Will I what?" DJ brought her mind back to the present.

"Darla Jean, please pay attention. This is extremely important."

DJ nodded.

"I am asking you to agree to see your father. He would like to come here to visit."

"I don't have to go to his house?"

"No, not until you want to."

"What if I don't ever want to?" The urge to chew her fingernails made DJ bite her bottom lip instead.

"I don't know yet what the legal ramifications might be. The way the laws read today, Brad could force the issue." Lindy rubbed her head again. A lock of hair swung forward on her left cheek, and she absentmindedly pushed the wayward hair back over her ear.

"Mom, he never paid any attention to us all these years. How come he can just drop in and make me see him?"

"I don't know." Lindy looked her daughter full in the face. "DJ, have I ever said anything to make you hate your father?"

DJ shook her head. "We never even talked about him. I guess I figured he died or something. I liked our life the way it was—Gran and you and me. I never needed a dad."

"But didn't you question why we never mentioned him?"

"Once or twice I wondered, but it was no big deal." DJ sank into the soft wing chair that had always been Gran's. "Guess I thought more about getting a horse than getting a dad." She studied the cuticle on her right forefinger. *I will not bite it off. I can do all things*. "What does Robert say about all this?"

"He's the one who suggested you see Brad."

"Tell him thanks a big fat bunch. I thought he wanted to be my dad."

"He did and he does. Nothing has changed there. He and the boys are coming over for dinner tomorrow as a matter of fact." When DJ groaned, she added, "Robert's bringing the dinner."

"Oh, good, then. I don't have time to cook and neither do you. And if this rain doesn't let up, I'll be so far behind in jumping Major, I'll have to start all over again."

"So you'll see Brad?" Her mother hung on to the subject like a starving dog to a bone.

"All right!" DJ wrinkled her forehead and thumped her hands on the arms of her chair. "But I don't have to like him."

"But you'll be polite." It wasn't a question.

DJ stuck her finger in her mouth and bit off the troublesome cuticle snag.

"DJ."

She made a face. Now her finger stung, and she could see blood rising to the surface. She sighed. "Yes, Mother, I will be polite. When is he coming?"

"Sunday afternoon."

"Sunday afternoon! Why didn't you check with me first? If it's not raining, I want that time to work Major."

"This is slightly more important than one workout."

"That's what you—" DJ clamped her mouth closed.

"I'm not asking you to sell your horse, for crying out loud. As important as this is, it will only take a couple of hours to do. Gran and Joe will be here, too."

"So Joe can beat him up?"

"Darla Jean Randall, if you would be so kind—"

"I'm leaving. I'll be in my room studying if you decide this is all a horrible mistake."

"Good night, DJ."

DJ climbed the stairs, feeling like she was dragging the world behind her. She glanced out her bedroom window and grew more discouraged. Rain pocked the miniature lake in their backyard and roared in their downspouts. Was this what Noah had felt like? How'd he handle forty days and nights like this?

She thought of an idea and barreled out of her room and down the stairs. "How about if I just call and talk with him? I could do that."

Lindy nodded. "That's a start. Then you can decide if you want him to come on Sunday or not."

"No question there," DJ muttered under her breath.

The next afternoon in English class, DJ groaned along with the rest of the kids.

"You want us to do what?" one of the boys moaned.

"You are all going to begin keeping journals. The purpose of this assignment is to write something every day to get in touch with what is going on inside of you."

"My insides want food."

The class snickered.

DJ felt like putting her head down on her desk and groaning, too. How was she going to write in a notebook every day? She had too much to do already. She tuned back in to what the teacher was saying.

"There are many ways of keeping journals. Famous people all through history have kept journals—it is one of the ways we know what life was like way back when. Thomas Jefferson kept a journal, as did Ben Franklin."

"How about some women?" asked a girl.

"Many did. There are collections of journals kept by the women who traveled the Oregon Trail. Abigail Adams never failed to write in hers. However, the one I want you all to read is more current than those and was written by a young girl about your age. When you read her journal, you will get an intimate picture of a Jewish girl hiding from the Nazis during World War II. There's a new version out now that contains entries not published in the earlier. Have any of you read *The Diary of Anne Frank*?

DJ raised her hand. Not too many others did.

"How many of you have seen the movie?"

DJ kept her hand up.

"Good." Mrs. Adams turned to the board to add some more instructions. "You will need a three-ring binder or a spiral notebook. I prefer to use a binder because I can add more pages as I need them, but a spiral-bound notebook is fine. Put your name on the front of the book and date each entry. I'll expect an entry for each day."

"How long do they have to be?" someone asked.

"As long as you want, just so you write more than one sentence a day. It's important that you write down how you feel about the day's events or anything else you might be thinking about."

"Right now I feel tired," the boy behind DJ whispered.

"But what if someone reads what I wrote?" another student asked.

"Hey, yeah. Are you going to read them?"

"Only if you want me to. I'll have you turn in your journal once a week at first, then if all is well, twice a month. All I am interested in is making sure you wrote every day." She looked at the girl who had brought up the privacy issue. "A journal is a very personal thing. I would not leave mine out for anyone to read, and if that's something that worries you, you may store your journal here in the bottom drawer of my desk and insert your pages as you go."

Great, how am I ever going to keep up with this assignment? I don't have anything to write about. DJ propped her forehead on her hand. What a bummer. *I can't keep track of all I'm doing already*. She swapped looks of disgust with the girl across the aisle. *What a stupid assignment*. She broke into her internal complaining long enough to listen to what the teacher was saying.

"I have copies of the older edition of *The Diary of Anne Frank,* but if you want to read the new one, you'll have to buy that for yourself at the local bookstore."

Fat chance. While DJ enjoyed reading, it usually took a backseat to riding and drawing. While other kids read, she drew horses.

"Now, I'd like you to take out your notebooks and begin

your first entry. Place the date in the left-hand margin and your name up in the right." Groans echoed around the room, but the class did as asked. "Good. Now, think of something that's been bothering you today. Did you have a fight with your brother or sister? Someone say something that ticked you off? Bad hair day?"

Giggles and raised eyebrows greeted her small joke.

"Whatever you feel like writing about, start in."

More groans.

DJ stared at her paper. What to write about? Her pencil began to move as if it had a mind of its own. *Last week I heard from my dad. I never even knew his name before, and now he wants to see me*. Before she knew it, the teacher called time. DJ looked down—she'd written three-quarters of a page.

By the time DJ turned her lights out that night, she'd covered four pages, both sides.

She didn't need her mother's questioning look to remind her that she'd said she would call her father. Every time she decided to pick up the phone, the butterflies in her midsection would go into a grand free-for-all. About the time she felt them halfway up her throat in a full-blown flight for freedom, she'd chicken out and they'd go back to roost.

What would she say? *Hey, come on down and let's be best buds?* Or *You come down, but I'll be gone*. Or better yet, *Gee, been a while since I saw you—if I ever did*. DJ knew none of those would earn points with her mother. Or Gran, for that matter. When she tried praying about it as Gran suggested, it was like talking into a phone when the other person had already hung up. There wasn't so much as a dial tone.

"Just do it and get it over with," Amy said, hands on her board-flat hips.

"Easy for you to say, you saw your father this morning." DJ held out a carrot to Josh, who took it daintily, as the sorrel Arab cross did everything. He and Amy were just right for each other, both small and neatly put together.

"What's that got to do with it?" Amy stopped brushing. "My mom says to just do the hard stuff first and get it over with. Then you'll like yourself better."

"At least your mom is married to your father." DJ rubbed the spot near the tip of Josh's ears that made him act half asleep.

"Yeah, I know." Amy started brushing again, the dust flying as she used both hands. "But you've been snorting over this for what seems like forever. Wouldn't it be easier just to get it over with?"

"What do I call him? Mr. Atwood? Bradley? Brad? And what if his wife answers the phone—if he even has a wife."

"You could call him Dad."

"He's *not* my dad." DJ's raised voice made Josh pull back against the crossties.

"Oh, really now?"

"Come on, Ames, Dad is for someone you like." She chewed on her bottom lip. "I'd rather say, 'hey you.' "

"DJ, I don't care what you call him, just do it quickly so you can concentrate on riding again—and school and drawing and anything else but this." Amy threw her brushes into the bucket. "Major's waiting for you."

"No, he's not. He doesn't want to go out in that downpour any more than I do." DJ glanced at her watch. "Yikes, I better hurry. Patches has been out on the hot walker long enough. Maybe the rain washed some of his orneriness away."

DJ had been scheduled for her first dressage lesson that afternoon, but Bridget had left a note asking DJ to forgive her; she had an unexpected appointment. They'd reschedule it for Saturday morning. Since she wasn't particularly looking forward to a dressage lesson—jumping was what she loved, not boring dressage—the postponement didn't hurt DJ's feelings. And when Patches semi-behaved himself, she actually dared to look forward to some play time with Major. Shame they couldn't ride up in the hills, but getting drenched had never been her idea of a great time.

DJ spent her time working at keeping Major bending and yielding to her legs as Bridget had shown her. He showed his impatience with the repeated drills by swishing his tail every once in a while. DJ wished she could do the same.

When Joe dropped her off at the dark house, she hunched her shoulders to keep her neck dry and dashed to the front door. The dark windows were no surprise. She wondered whether her father would be home yet. Did he work late, too?

Inside, the house smelled stale and silent, as if bemoaning the fact no one was home.

DJ flicked on the lights, turned on the stereo, and crossed the kitchen to the phone. The red light was blinking on the answering machine. She listened to the message for her mother and hit the save button. The light continued to blink.

DJ got a glass of water to wet her parched mouth. You'd think it was a hundred degrees outside, she was so thirsty. Then she had to make a run to the bathroom.

"All right, you're obviously just putting this off." She crossed again to the phone and dialed.

A deep male voice answered on the third ring. "Brad Atwood here."

DJ swallowed hard. She couldn't make any words come.

"Hello?"

7

DJ DROPPED THE PHONE BACK in the cradle, her heart hammering like she'd run a mile without taking a breath. She dashed to the sink for another glass of water. "You idiot! What's the matter with you?" She stared at the reflection in the kitchen window. No help there. The face looked about to cry. For Pete's sake!

She took in a deep breath and, letting it out, crossed to the phone again. Summoning every bit of resolution she owned clear up from her toenails, she dialed the number.

"Brad Atwood here."

"This is DJ."

"DJ, how wonderful." She could hear warmth spreading over his words like hot fudge on ice cream. "I'm so glad you called."

"Yeah, well . . ." *What do I say next?* She twirled the cord around her finger. "I . . ."

"I know this is awfully hard for you and a tremendous surprise. Maybe it would help if I told you some about me, then you tell me a little about you."

"Okay."

"At least you know my name," he said with a hint of a chuckle. "I live near Santa Rosa, and I'm an attorney. I don't have any other children, but I'm married and my wife's name is Jacqueline—Jackie to her friends. We both love horses. I raise and show Arabians for my hobby, and Jackie shows fourth-level dressage on her Hanoverian-Thoroughbred gelding named Lord Byron."

DJ sighed. "Wow."

"I hoped that might interest you. Your mother says you love horses, too."

"Gran said once that I got that from my dad."

"Yes, I think you did. So . . . now tell me about you."

DJ slid down the wall and crossed her legs at the ankles, the phone propped on her shoulder. "Where do you want me to start?"

"Wherever. I'm interested in everything."

"Like you said, I've always loved horses—started working at Briones Riding Academy when I was ten so I could take riding lessons. Just this past summer, I got my own horse, Major. He's a retired police mount. I'm a freshman at Acalanese High School, I love to draw like Gran, and someday I want to ride in the Olympics."

"Dressage, eventing, or jumping?"

"Jumping." DJ could hear the interest in his voice. "I've always wanted to jump."

"You have a trainer?"

"Yep, Bridget Sommersby. She used to ride for France till she got hurt and couldn't jump anymore. She owns the academy where I work and train."

DJ heard a car pull into the drive and the garage door go up. "Mom's home, you want to talk with her?"

"I'd rather talk with you. I'm hoping you will let me come to see you."

"When?"

"Whenever. Your mother had mentioned Sunday, but I'll leave it to you to set the time and day."

DJ nibbled on the side of her lower lip and let out a breath she didn't realize she'd been holding. "How about three o'clock a week from this coming Sunday?"

"That's nine days from now. Good—we'll be there. Can you give me directions?"

DJ gave him the address and started to add directions.

"No need," Brad said. "That's the house your mother always lived in. We'll see you a week from Sunday, DJ—and thanks."

DJ hung up the phone as her mother walked into the kitchen. "That was Mr. Atwood."

Lindy stopped short. "Brad's father?"

DJ shook her head. "No, *my* father. You're always telling me to call adults mister and missus." DJ twisted the phone cord again. "What *am* I supposed to call him, Mom?" She glared up at her mother. "I don't know who he is or what he's like or anything. What am I supposed to do?" She rose to her feet, hot anger rising with her. "He wants to come see me. What do I say? 'Hi, Daddy, so nice to meet you'? Do I shake his hand? And his wife—I . . . I forget her name." DJ choked on her words.

Lindy stepped forward and wrapped her arms around her daughter. "It's okay, Darla Jean. I promise it'll be all right. You don't have to see him right now if you don't want to." Her voice sounded so much like Gran's that DJ snuggled closer.

"They're coming in nine days." She muttered the words against her mother's shoulder. Never in her life could she remember her mother comforting her like this. Gran had always been there first.

DJ inhaled the fragrance imbedded in the fabric and her mother's skin. It spoke of class and success and beautiful people in fascinating places, but her mother's arms and tone spoke only of love. "Is that okay?"

"If that's what you feel you're up to."

"Gran could make cookies." DJ didn't feel ready to step back from the comfort surrounding her.

Lindy nodded. "Brad always was a sucker for her chocolate chip peanut butter cookies."

"Gran doesn't make chocolate chip with peanut butter." DJ raised her head.

"She used to, and I'm sure she'd do it again. Guess she quit making that particular recipe after . . . after . . ."

"After he went away?"

Lindy clasped her hands on her daughter's upper arms. "I think we need to have a long talk." She sighed. "A long-overdue talk."

"Like about my dad?" DJ tried on a smile and found it still fit.

"Yeah, I kind of blew that one." Lindy put a finger under DJ's chin and lifted it so they were eye to eye. "Darla Jean Randall, I know I haven't been the kind of mother you needed and I should have been, but I promise you, I will try to do my best from here on in. I am just eternally grateful Gran was always there for you. She raised a young woman I am proud to call my daughter." Lindy's words caught in her throat. She cleared it and added, "So proud." The tears pooling in her eyes spilled over and matched the ones on DJ's cheeks. Her mother sniffed and smiled, a wobbly smile, but a smile nonetheless. "I love you, DJ, more than I can ever say." With gentle fingers, she wiped away the tears slipping down DJ's face.

"Oh, Mom." DJ tried to say more, but the words wouldn't come. She sniffed, too. "I smell like horses."

"That's okay—for now." Lindy reached behind her for a paper towel to wipe her eyes. "How about we both change clothes, and I'll order in." She stopped. "You want Chinese or pizza?"

"Pizza. With everything."

"Even anchovies?" Lindy raised one eyebrow.

DJ scrunched her eyes closed. She sighed as if making a big sacrifice. "How about on half?"

"Deal." Her mother extended her hand. DJ took it, and they shook once. "How about you order and I'll pay?"

"Deal." As Lindy climbed the stairs, DJ felt the laughter of pure joy swirl around her ankles and work its way upward. Pushing bubbles of thanks ahead, it burst out in feet-tapping, hand-clapping giggles and spins. "Wow!" If only Gran could see them now.

DJ phoned in the order and raced up the stairs. She had twenty minutes to shower and get dressed. A bit later, still damp from the pounding water, she stood in front of her closet. If only she had a lounging outfit like the ones her mother wore so easily. And beautifully.

"What?" She couldn't stop talking to herself. The energy had to come out somehow. "You want to dress up?" She shook her head. "DJ, you're slipping and slipping bad." She dug out her Snoopy nightshirt, a bathrobe that was now too short in the sleeves, and shoved her feet into fluffy Snoopy slippers. At least she'd be warm while they talked. And man, oh man, did she have questions to ask!

With the pizza box between them, they curled into the corners of the sofa in the family room.

"So how do I start?" Lindy asked after eating half a piece of pizza.

"Gran always says to start at the beginning." DJ scooped up a string of cheese and plopped it back on the pizza.

"She's right." Lindy took a sip from her soda and leaned back. "I had a crush on Brad Atwood from the first day I saw him in high school. He was so handsome, every girl in the hall drooled when he walked by. The first time he said hi to me, I nearly dropped my books." A gentle smile lifted the corners of her mouth, and her eyes wore the dreamy look of good memories. "And when he asked me to go to a movie, I about flipped."

"How old were you?"

"Fifteen."

"Gran let you go out on a date at fifteen?" DJ couldn't believe it.

"It wasn't really a *date* date—a bunch of kids were going." Lindy reached for another piece of pizza. "But *I* was going with the BMOC."

" 'BMOC'?"

"Big Man On Campus."

DJ stifled the *huh?* and took a sip of her drink. *They did talk kinda funny back in the old days.* When her mother seemed lost in her daydreams, DJ prodded, "And then?"

"Well," Lindy shrugged. "We started going together. Mom and Dad had a fit when they learned I was going steady with Brad. He was too old for me, too fast for me. I was too young, couldn't think of anything but boys . . . but you need to remember, I was only interested in one boy—Brad Atwood." Her face sobered. "Even though my mother and father did their best to keep their little girl safe, Brad and I—well, we were in love, and eventually we . . ." Her voice trailed off.

DJ waited, not daring to say a word.

Lindy sat up straight and crossed her wrists on her knees. She stared at a spot on the rug in front of her. "Let's just say we went all the way."

"You mean you had sex?"

"We thought we were making love, and what we made was a baby. Two kids too stupid to use birth control and too much in love or lust to keep away from each other." Lindy's voice ground to a halt. The ticking clock on the mantel sounded loud in the stillness. Out on the street, a car swished through the water drenching the road from the continuing rain. "If only I had listened to my mother." The words were almost lost behind her fall of hair.

"When I told him I was pregnant, Brad said he'd marry me—said he loved me and he'd stand by me." Lindy shook her head. "His father thought I should have an abortion. Can you beat that—he thought I should kill the baby?" She stared at DJ out of haunted eyes. "He would have had me kill *you.*" She raised a trembling hand to DJ's cheek. "I couldn't do that. My own dad thought I should give you up for adoption so I could get on with my life. But when I decided to keep you, he and Mom said there was always room for one more in this house. We were a family that stuck together. So we did."

She kept her gaze locked on DJ's. "When I held you in my arms and you looked up at me, that was it. I'd been talking to you for weeks, and suddenly you were real and I couldn't let you go."

"What happened to Brad?" DJ could barely get the words past the lump in her throat.

"You've got to give him some credit—he paid the medical bills. But while I was taking care of a newborn baby and trying to go to night school, he played football and basketball and tried out for track. Back then, they wouldn't let you attend high school if you were pregnant or had a baby. When he left for college, he said we'd be married as soon as he graduated. . . ." Her voice trailed off again.

But did he care about me at all? Did he play with me? Was he a dad? DJ kept the questions to herself. And waited.

Lindy shook her head. "I was so mad at the whole world, I can't believe my family put up with me. My friends were out having a good time—the dances, the dates—and me?" She shook her head again, so gently now her hair didn't even swing. "DJ, I was so young, I didn't know how to be a mother. I was just a kid myself. So I went back to school to learn a skill so I could get a job, and Gran took over with you. We didn't do welfare then like kids do now."

"I know a girl who had an abortion," DJ volunteered.

"Yeah, and she may not know it now, but it will haunt her for the rest of her life." Lindy turned so she could look directly at DJ. "I know I made mistakes, but keeping you was never one of them. I'm sorry Brad missed out on your growing-up years, but that was his choice. He just faded out of the picture."

"And now he wants to come back in."

"I know."

It was DJ's turn to lean forward. There were so many questions she wanted to ask. *Did you ever wish I wasn't here? Did you hate Brad? Do you hate him now?* "You weren't much older than me." The stunning thought swung her around.

"I know. And I hope you never get boy crazy like I did. Poor Gran, it about drove her nuts. Looking back, all I could think about, talk about, and dream about was Brad Atwood."

He could have come to see me—at least once. It wasn't as if we'd moved to New York or something. We still live in the same house my mother grew up in. He even remembers where it is.

"Do you have any pictures of him?"

Lindy shook her head. "I burned them all one night when I heard he took some other girl to the prom."

Silence fell again, this time more like a warm blanket. Lindy gathered up the napkins and closed the pizza box on the remaining piece. "You want this?"

"For breakfast." DJ slumped against the sofa back. "You know what bugs me the most?"

Lindy shook her head.

"Why now?"

"Guess you'll have to ask him that."

"Are you still mad at him?"

"I wasn't until he crashed back into our lives. Now I'm angry with him at times—more times than I want to admit."

"Me too." DJ rubbed the scar in the palm of her hand and sighed. "Thanks, Mom."

"You're welcome, DJ. Sweet dreams," Lindy said as they climbed the stairs to their bedrooms.

"You too." DJ stepped into her mother's embrace just like they'd been hugging all her life. "Night."

But for the second night since DJ had learned of Brad Atwood, she awoke in the dark of the night, panting hard—running from a faceless man.

8

SEVEN DAYS TILL D-DAY, but who's counting? DJ stared at the words she'd written in her journal and chewed on the eraser of her pencil before writing some more. *Sometimes I think I hate him and hope he doesn't show up. Then I'm scared he won't come. What if I don't like him, or he doesn't like me? Then what?*

Her fingers itched to draw instead of write, but she forced herself to keep at it. She flipped back a couple of pages. She'd written all she could remember her mother saying about her early life. One section in particular caught her attention. *"My own dad thought I should give the baby up for adoption so I could get on with my life, but when I held you in my arms and you looked up at me, that was it. I'd been talking to you for weeks, and suddenly you were real and I couldn't let you go."*

DJ felt a shiver ripple up her back. What if she'd been given away?

She forced her attention back to the current entry. *I wonder what he looks like one minute, then the next, I'm so scared. Scared one minute and mad the next. I think I'm having a nervous breakdown. Do crazy people think like this? Gran says to pray about it like she is, but it's so hard. And what about his wife? What if she doesn't like me? Fourth-*

level dressage—major wow. And if they are horse people, how can I not like them? Dear God, please help me.

Oh, and please make Bridget change her mind. Today she said I should take two dressage lessons a week and no jumping lessons for a couple of months. I mean, jumping is what I want to do. I understand learning dressage can make me a better rider, but can't I jump, too? It's not like I plan to show dressage or anything. Please, God, you know Bridget—only you can change her mind.

DJ finally put away her journal pages and took out her drawing pad. After sharpening her pencils, her fingers seemed to take on a life of their own as they shaped a horse on the paper. She held the sketch of the jumping horse up to the light when she finished. Definitely Major. She'd gotten his head just right, but his rear legs were slightly off. When would she draw him right?

She rubbed a hand across her forehead. Mom was out with Robert. They'd gone over to look at the new house and see how the remodeling was coming. It was too late to call Amy, and Gran and Joe were at a meeting. She picked up her journal again.

THIS JUST ISN'T FAIR!!! DJ underlined the capitalized words three times, pushing so hard the lead on her pencil broke. She stuffed the pages in her folder and slipped the folder into her backpack. Dumping the thing on the floor, she reached to turn out the light. But when sleep came, the faceless man came with it.

They finally had sunshine the next afternoon. DJ checked the jumping ring. Still wet but not sloppy. She ached to jump a round—or ten.

"I know, ma petite, but your time in the ring is so short now that winter is here that I believe dressage is best."

"Whoa, you scared me." DJ turned to find Bridget Sommersby at her shoulder. "How'd you know I'd be out here?" Even scarier, how did Bridget know what she was thinking?

Bridget just smiled. With her ash blond hair in a neat bun at her neck and her glasses resting a bit above her hairline, she looked the picture of the neat horsewoman. Blue eyes, crinkles at their outer edges, smiled along with the instructor's lips. "You will like dressage eventually, and even if you do not, you are enough of a horsewoman to see the value in it. Go ahead and finish your work. I will join you and Major in the arena."

DJ nodded. So much for God answering that particular prayer with a yes.

By the time she'd groomed and worked Patches, given her student Andrew his lesson, and saddled Major, she still hadn't mustered any more enthusiasm for her dressage lesson—especially after seeing Tony Andrada taking the jumps. *I should be out there.*

"Come on, Major, let's get warmed up. I don't think you are going to like this any more than I am." The bay snorted and tossed his head, jigged to the side, and struck out with one front foot. "You like the sun, too, don't you? We could have gone up into the hills today. Oh, why didn't I think of that?" DJ stroked his neck and leaned over to open the gate. "Maybe it'll be nice Saturday so we can go."

"Go where?" Amy jogged by on Josh.

"Up in Briones."

"I'm ready." She stopped her mount so DJ could close the gate. "You ready for your lesson?"

"Don't remind me. I could be out jumping—it's the first time in weeks the ring is dry enough."

"Bridget knows best."

"Thanks for taking her side." By the time DJ had circled the arena three times, Bridget had opened the gate and walked to one end. DJ nudged Major into a trot and, following Bridget's beckoning hand, stopped in front of her.

"All right, DJ, we will begin. First, I want to remind you that our goal is to make you a better rider and Major a more athletic horse. I can promise you will become a better jumper because you are willing to work with dressage. Understand?"

DJ nodded.

"Good. Then let us start with the basics. First, you must learn to sit straight. You are used to leaning forward, which is right for Hunter/Jumper. But you will sit straight for dressage." She looked up at DJ.

DJ straightened her shoulders and tried to visualize a straight line from her ear to her heel.

Bridget reached up and pushed her upper body back even more. "I said straight."

"I was."

"Non." Bridget shook her head. "Straight till you feel you are leaning backward. Now, do not let your leg swing forward."

DJ bit back the *I am straight* and tried to sit even straighter. She felt like she was leaning so far back her head rested on Major's rump.

"That is better. Now, signal Major to walk and hold your position."

DJ obeyed, stiff as a board and off balance.

"Now, relax."

Oh, sure, relax. Easy to say, impossible to do. DJ gritted her teeth. How was she supposed to watch where she was going when she couldn't even turn her head?

"Now then." Bridget beckoned DJ back to halt in front of her. "Take your feet out of the stirrups." DJ did as told. With swift motions, Bridget pulled the leather buckles of the stirrups' down straps and laid the irons over the front of the saddle, right first, then left.

"What are you doing?"

"You have to learn to feel your horse in three places, your two seat bones and in front in the crotch. When you are sitting so straight and deep that you can feel your mount move beneath you, you will come along quickly." Bridget smiled up at DJ. "Feeling comfortable yet?"

"No, not at all."

"Walk, please."

Yeah, sure—walk. This feels totally weird. Major twitched his ears. "Sorry, fella."

"And trot sitting."

If this was what a sack of grain felt like, DJ figured they could call her "oats" for short. What had happened to her balance? She felt herself slip from side to side. She was riding more clumsily than the first time she had gotten on a horse.

Major swished his tail and stopped. A dead stop. The only problem was DJ didn't. Until she hit the dirt, that is.

At least she had the presence of mind to release the reins so she didn't jerk Major's mouth. He looked down at her, then nuzzled her shoulder as if to apologize.

"Of all the stupid—"

"It is all right. You are learning." Bridget came over and gave DJ a hand to pull her to her feet.

"I fell off—just like some little kid. He didn't dump me." Major nuzzled her again. "Sorry, guy, it wasn't your fault." She rubbed his ears and smoothed his forelock, then turned to Bridget. "Okay, so what did I do wrong?"

"Nothing. Major stopped because you were doing what I told you to do. Without even knowing, you were sitting deeper. Now, if you would have used your legs to drive the horse forward, you would still be on him."

DJ grumbled to herself as she pulled her left stirrup down so she could mount. Once aboard, she flipped the stirrup back in front of her. *I will do this!*

"Let us keep to the walk."

By the end of the lesson, DJ ached in places she'd forgotten she had. Besides being dumped on her rear, her seat hurt from the constant contact with the saddle. Her inner thighs hurt from trying to keep them flat against the saddle skirt. And her pride hurt from jouncing around like a bag of horse feed.

"You did well." Bridget patted DJ's knee.

"Yeah, sure."

"And you will practice?"

"Of course." DJ gave her a who-you-kidding look.

"Good. You might try a hot bath when you get home. Helps the sore places." Bridget opened the gate and waved her through.

"You okay, kid?" Joe asked when she and Major arrived back at the stall.

"You saw?"

Joe nodded. "Looked to me like she was trying to torture you."

"That about fits it. Think I'll change to Western." DJ slid to the ground and leaned against her horse. Major turned so he could rub his head against her shoulder. "Easy, fella, you'll knock me over."

She stripped off the saddle and pad and hung them on the top edge of the lower stall door. Then, after hooking the halter around Major's neck, she removed the bridle and laid it over the saddle. How come even her arms ached?

"Here, let me help." Joe unhooked the web gate, picked the brushes out of the bucket, and began a two-handed grooming job that would leave Major shining in no time.

"But, GJ, you already cleaned the stall and put out the feed," DJ tried to protest. She was glad for the help. How come she could jump or even do flat work for hours and not feel drained like this? What was she going to say when her father's wife, whatever her name was again, asked about the dressage lessons? *Just great. I only fell off once.*

"DJ, don't take it so hard. You know that riders fall off plenty of times. It's all part of the sport." Joe grinned at her. "Or at least that's what I heard you telling your students."

"I know. It's just so embarrassing. I wasn't even galloping or jumping or anything—just trotting. The kids I'm teaching stay on better than I did." DJ finished buckling Major's halter after giving him the last chunk of carrot.

"It'll get better." Joe dropped the brushes in the bucket and took her arm. "Come on, I know Melanie was baking cookies when I left. I think you could use a good dose of cookies and Gran."

By the time DJ wrote about the disastrous lesson in her journal, she was able to laugh, although barely. She probably had looked pretty silly, grabbing for the air and collapsing like a rag doll. Even Major had looked at her as though he wondered what he'd done wrong. As Gran had said, "Someday you'll laugh when you tell your children about this first dressage lesson."

But would she ever be able to laugh about the day she met her father?

Meeting him is always in the back of my mind now, she wrote. *I can't wait until that day is over. I know Mom is pretty uptight about it, too. I heard her talking to Robert, and she was crying. I don't know why she's so worried. This won't change her life much, just mine. But then again, maybe we'll meet and he'll go his way and I'll go mine.*

But is that what I really want? She tapped the eraser of her pencil against her chin. Always more questions.

"So what are you doing about Christmas presents this year?" Amy asked one afternoon. They were riding their bikes to the Academy for a change since it wasn't raining. In fact, it hadn't rained for a couple of days.

"I don't know. My saddle fund keeps shrinking—at this rate I'll be fifty before I can afford a decent, all-purpose saddle, let alone a good jumping saddle. What are you going to do?"

"I'm thinking of enlarging some of my photos and framing them. John said he'd help me make frames in wood shop."

"Must be nice sometimes to have an older brother."

"Yeah, sometimes. Other times I'd give him away in a heartbeat."

"I already gave Gran and Joe one of my drawings for the wedding, so I can't do that again." They stopped at the top of the hill and waited for several cars to go by.

"You could for some of the others."

"I guess, but frames cost a bundle, and I don't have John to help me out. One thing about having more family now, I've got more presents to buy."

"I still think you ought to be able to do something with your drawings."

"But what?"

"I don't know. Ask Gran."

"Oh, sure, 'Hey, Gran, what do you want me to make you for Christmas?' " They propped their bikes against the barn wall and headed over to the office to check the duties board. Since neither of their names were down for cleaning stalls, they heaved a collective sigh of relief.

"Have you two drawn names out of the bowl for the Christmas party?" Bridget called from her office.

DJ groaned. "Another present. I think I'm going to get a job at the Burger House."

"Yeah, in your spare time." Amy put her hand in the

glass fish bowl and drew out a slip of white paper.

DJ did the same and groaned again.

"Now what?"

DJ held out the narrow strip for inspection. "Tony Andrada. Fiddle and double fiddle. Who'd you get?"

"Sue Benson. No problema."

"Bridget, can I trade this name for another?" DJ put on her most imploring look. "Please."

With a slight smile, the academy owner shook her head. "You know the rules. Oh, and, DJ, Andrew will not be in for his lesson today. He has a bad cold."

"Probably got it so he wouldn't have to groom Bandit. I'd hoped to get him mounted today."

"Did you tell him that?"

"You kidding? But he's no dummy. He's learned to tack the pony up and lead him around. He might be driving a car before I get him on that horse."

"I know you work hard with him, and his mother appreciates the care you have shown. Shame he is so frightened."

"Shame they don't let him play soccer or something instead."

"Facing your fears is very important and part of growing up."

"Yeah, well, *I'm* afraid I won't have presents for Christmas." DJ stuck her hands in her windbreaker pockets. "See ya later." She turned and headed out the door, knowing full well that she hadn't mentioned what she was really afraid of—meeting her father.

That night, she took out her portfolio of her best pencil and charcoal drawings and studied each one. While many of them were of Major, she had foals, yearlings, and horses jumping, walking, grazing, and lying down. The one of a horse rearing wasn't quite right, and she flipped past it quickly. She also flipped past the drawings she'd added riders to—she was better with horses than people. While she'd been tempted to throw out the sketches from her early years, Gran had told her to keep them so she could see how she'd grown. Her growth as an artist was obvious, even though the subject matter was limited to horses.

DJ turned out the light. Only three days until D-day. And only fourteen more days to figure out Christmas presents.

9

"ARE YOU OKAY?"

DJ looked up at her mother waiting in the doorway. "Yeah, why?"

"You've been so quiet lately." Lindy motioned to ask if she could come in, and DJ patted the edge of her bed. "Is it about your dad?"

"Sorta." DJ pushed away her art pad, flipped over on her back, and studied her mother. As always, Lindy looked like she'd just stepped out of a fashion magazine. Her emerald green silk lounging outfit whispered secrets as she sat down and turned to rest one knee on the comforter.

"What do you mean by 'sorta'?"

DJ sighed. "For starters, what do I call him?" She crossed one ankle over her other knee.

"Mr. Atwood seems kind of weird, doesn't it?" Lindy said, nodding. "And you can't call him Brad because Gran and I would have a fit."

Lindy laid a comforting hand on DJ's shoulder, sending shock waves through her. "I can see why this would be a problem for you." More shock waves. *Is this my mother?*

"I guess if it were me, I'd be pretty mad at him sometimes, even might think I hate him." Lindy's voice had that gentle quality DJ used with Andrew when she was trying to get him over being afraid of Bandit. "You been thinking that?"

The question caught DJ by surprise. "Yeah, I guess so."

"Gran thought you might, but you haven't really said much." Lindy's hand continued to stroke DJ's shoulder. "Robert and I talked about it, you know. He wondered what you were thinking and feeling." Silence. "You care to talk about it?"

The words came in a whisper. "I'm so scared, Mom . . . so scared."

"Makes sense. Me too."

DJ stopped in midthought. "Why are you scared?"

"You first."

"Well, I . . . I don't know. It's just all so sudden. I mean, we were fine without him, and now all of a sudden he's there and wants to be a part of my life—at least I think so. Sometimes I get so mad at him." DJ flipped back over on her stomach. "Why can't things stay the way they've always been?"

"That's life, honey—change and more change. Lately more than ever—and mostly because I met this neat man I thought my mother would enjoy being with." Lindy clasped her hands around a knee. "Shoulda just kept my mouth shut."

"Gran's really happy being married to Joe." DJ toyed with her pencil. "I wouldn't want to change that."

"Even though you miss her?"

"Yep. I get along okay." DJ drew circles on the comforter with her finger. "And I really like Joe, you know that."

"So change isn't always so bad?"

DJ let the question sink in. Growing up was change. She'd always wanted to ride and draw better—that was change, too. And Robert and her mother getting married, now that would be the biggest change of all. With the Double Bs around, nothing would ever be the same again. Did she not want that to happen?

She curled onto her side so she could see her mother. Her mother had sure been different lately—softer, more smiling, and even open to talking with her once in a while. Would she want that to go back to the old way? "Guess not, at least not all the time."

DJ thought a minute. "Do you want to see him again?"

"Who, Brad?"

DJ nodded.

"Not particularly. That part of my life is like a book I closed a long time ago. I like looking ahead." Lindy rumpled DJ's hair. "We'll get through this, and Christmas isn't far away. How you coming with your presents?"

DJ was glad for the new topic. "I'm stuck. We have so much more family now."

"Ain't that the truth." She leaned forward and picked up DJ's drawing pad. "You mind?"

DJ shook her head. She watched her mother's face as she flipped through the sheets. Lindy smiled, chuckled at the colt illustrations, and nodded once or twice.

"DJ, you sure inherited your grandmother's talent. Some of these are really good. You ever thought about choosing one or two and reducing them down to card size? These would make neat note cards."

"I could make up a package of six or eight." DJ felt her brain spring to attention and start working. "They wouldn't have to all be different." DJ took back her drawing pad and started flipping through. "This one, I think." She pointed at the side view of a foal. "And this one." A cameo of Major, ears pricked, made her grin.

"You have plenty to choose from." Lindy leaned forward. "Good night, DJ. Time to hit the sack." She dropped a kiss on her daughter's head and stood to leave. "Don't worry about meeting your biological father. Things are always worse when you are anticipating them."

DJ nodded. "Sure, Mom."

The next morning when she told Amy about the cards, Amy lit up like a neon sign. "I could do the same with some of my photos. Shame it's too late, we might have been able to sell some of these."

"You're right." The wheels began to turn. "We could buy the envelopes and—"

"You two going to make another business flier?" Mr. Yamamoto asked as he braked for a stoplight.

"Flier?" DJ looked at Amy. "We don't need more fliers—we did that last summer."

"No, I mean a new venture. You've had some good ideas in the past, they just—"

"D-a-d," Amy moaned. "You don't have to remind us."

"Good thing those hamsters didn't get loose at *our* house is all I've got to say." John sank down in the seat. "Mom would've gone ballistic."

"My mom about did." DJ grinned at Amy. "At least with cards, they can't escape or track horse manure on someone's brand-new white carpet." That had happened during the Pony Parties venture, when DJ and Amy had used Bandit to give kids rides at parties. "Gotta admit, though, those Pony Parties were our best idea of all. Ames, we should do that again."

"Count me out." John gathered his gear. "I'm not helping with something like that ever again."

DJ and Amy exchanged grins. "Thanks for the ride, Dad," DJ sang out as they exited the car. John disappeared into the throng of teenagers. "So, Ames, when you want to go to the Copy Shop?"

Sunday afternoon arrived faster than anyone was ready for.

"I can't stand it—I think I'm going to be sick." DJ made a puking motion toward the sink.

"Darla Jean Randall, act your age."

"Now, dear, you know she's only teasing." This was already the third time Gran had acted as peacemaker.

"No, I'm not teasing. I've got butterflies on my butterflies. This is worse than a competition any day." DJ opened the refrigerator door and studied the contents. Nothing looked appetizing, and Gran had already smacked her hands away from the cookie platter with a stern warning.

"Close the door, you'll cool the entire house." Lindy's voice said more than her words. It said, Knock it off, DJ, I'm losing my patience. But then, Lindy hadn't had much patience for the last two days.

DJ felt as if she were dancing on the end of a low-voltage wire. Even Gran couldn't calm her down.

Maybe the Atwoods won't come. Maybe they won't find our place after all. And maybe DJ ought to go for a forty-mile run. She opened the fridge again and this time retrieved a can of soda.

"DJ, I said to stay out of there." Lindy whirled from where she was starting the coffee maker. The *kerthwunk* of an open coffee can hitting the floor caught everyone's attention.

"Lindy Lou Randall!" Gran only used that tone when her daughter resorted to the kind of language that had just turned the air blue. "Get a hold of yourself."

"Look, you three women go about your business, and I'll clean up the coffee." Joe gently laid a hand on Melanie's shoulder.

"Thank you, darlin'." Gran placed her hand over his. "I'll go check the table." She glared at her daughter, shot her granddaughter a lesser glare, and headed for the dining room.

"Lindy, come here a minute, please," Robert called from the family room.

DJ watched her mother fix a smile on her face and, after one last laser look leveled at her daughter, leave the room.

"Where's the broom?" Joe asked, picking up the now half-empty coffee can. Dark brown ground coffee covered a sizable portion of the kitchen floor.

"I'll get it." DJ opened the door to the garage and snagged the broom off its hook. All this because she'd gotten a soda? Gran never got mad, or rarely anyway. But she'd definitely been mad a couple of minutes ago. DJ handed the broom to Joe and went back for the dustpan.

After they'd cleaned up the mess, he winked at her. "Don't take it too hard. Everyone's under pressure here."

"Why are they so worried? It's me who has to meet him. At least they know the guy," DJ whispered back.

"There's a lot at stake here, that's why." Joe leaned against the counter and crossed his arms over his chest.

"Yeah, well, I'd rather be at the barn. What a waste of good riding time."

"It'll be dark soon."

"There are lights in the arena."

"But you never ride after dark."

"Not in the winter, but I would if I could." DJ copied his pose.

"It's pouring again."

"So what's new? Maybe God's trying to wash California off the map."

The doorbell rang.

DJ could feel her heart pounding somewhere down near her knees.

"This is it, darlin'," Joe whispered with a light brush of his knuckles across her cheek. "Knock 'em dead."

DJ listened to her mother cross the room, her heels clicking on the entry tile. The door squeaked when she opened it. Lindy's voice sounded as if she'd just put on her best company manners for someone she didn't like at all.

"Hello, Brad, won't you come in?"

DJ shot a pleading look at her grandfather, who gave her a gentle push forward.

The voices continued. A man's voice, deep and smooth. Would Brad be as nice as his voice? He introduced his wife, Jacquelyn, and Lindy introduced Robert as her fiancé. Gran returned to the kitchen and, wrapping a comforting arm around DJ's waist, began walking her toward the group in the entry.

"Hello, Bradley, so good to see you again." Gran kept her one arm around DJ while she extended her other hand.

"Mrs. Randall, you haven't changed a bit." Bradley Atwood took her hand in both of his.

DJ sucked in her breath. Her father looked like a movie star. Hair a bit darker than hers, waved back off a broad forehead, and a male version of the determined jaw she saw in the mirror every morning. On him it looked good. His smile reached his eyes, the kind of smile you couldn't help but return. While he wasn't as tall as Joe, DJ had to tip her head back to look up at him.

"And this is Darla Jean, but if you want her to like you, call her DJ." Gran's soft voice interrupted DJ's study.

"Hi, DJ, I'm right glad to meet you." His voice cracked, then smoothed out. Light from the fixture above made his eyes sparkle—or was it tears that threatened to choke both his throat and his eyes?

She couldn't have answered if her life depended upon it.

He dropped his gaze and, turning slightly, said, "I'd like

you to meet my wife, Jacquelyn."

Come on, yo-yo brain, say something. DJ could still feel Gran's arm around her waist, strong and comforting.

"H-hi, I'm pleased to meet you." Her voice came breathy, as though she'd been running. She hoped the smile she'd ordered had arrived. She wanted to run, to jump, to yell. She wanted to go hide in her closet and not come out till they left.

"Come, we don't need to stand here. The coffee's ready, and we can visit much more easily around the dining room table." Gran motioned everyone toward the dining room and hung back for Lindy to lead the way.

Later, when DJ had played the scene over for the umpteenth time, she could see the look in her mother's eyes. It hadn't been very friendly. And Joe hadn't been his usual self either. In fact, without Gran, everyone would have been terribly uncomfortable—DJ especially. But Gran had been Gran, asking questions, telling stories of earlier years, passing around the chocolate chip peanut butter cookies that Brad praised to the skies.

As her mother had said, "I guess it went okay."

As far as DJ was concerned, the best part was talking about horses. Brad had asked about Major and what she did at the Academy, then told her about their Arabians and some of the places they'd showed.

Man, oh man, did she have a lot to tell Amy in the morning! DJ dug out her journal and began writing. She wanted to be sure to remember every little detail. *At least Bradley Atwood and I have plenty to talk about*, she finished writing. *That's for sure*.

She was just dropping off to sleep when she remembered something she'd overheard her mother saying to Gran. What was it again? Something about silver-tongued lawyers always getting their way. What was that supposed to mean? All he'd said was that he'd call her. What on earth was bugging her mother now?

"IF YOU HAD TONY ANDRADA TO BUY FOR, what would you buy?"

"I wouldn't have Tony Andrada for all the money in the world." Amy licked chocolate pudding from the back of her spoon as a crumpled milk carton whizzed by her left ear. She turned and glared over her shoulder at the guys at the table behind them. "You'd think the teachers could keep better control in the lunchroom."

"Ames, you're not helping."

"Give him a packet of your note cards."

"Oh, sure. The Neanderthal probably can't even write." DJ dug the last chip out of the sack. "I hate buying presents when I don't really know the person."

"You hate to *buy* anything. You put every dime in your saddle fund."

"I wish. My fund just gets flatter."

"Be glad you're buying a flat saddle then."

DJ groaned. "Now that's a real knee slapper." She smashed her lunch refuse together. "Just for that, you have to go shopping with me."

"If he was a little kid, you could give him a box of Lifesavers or something. That's what I gave Sue."

"I suppose you have all your Christmas shopping done, too."

"Of course." They dumped their trash into the container and headed for their lockers.

"Sometimes you make me sick." DJ pointed at her open mouth and made a gagging motion.

"I don't like leaving things to the last minute, not like some people I know."

"How far are you on your term paper?"

"Set to rewrite."

DJ groaned. "I just started writing. The research took up till now." DJ leaned her forehead against the tan metal locker. "Sometimes I hate school—it just takes away from the time I could be riding or drawing. And now I gotta go shopping, too."

"You better get on it because the party is Saturday night."

The bell rang. "Don't remind me," DJ muttered.

When Mrs. Adams returned DJ's journal that afternoon, she had written, *Glad to see you are racking up the pages. It shows this is helpful for you. Keep going.* DJ looked up to catch Mrs. Adams's eye and shared a smile with her. Now, if she could only get her term paper done on time.

That afternoon at the Academy, Andrew made it for his lesson. They had Bandit all groomed, and DJ was mentally preparing herself for the challenge of actually getting the ten-year-old on the pony.

"Okay, Andrew, this is the big day." DJ turned to the boy she'd been working with for the last few months. His mother, Mrs. Johnson, owned Patches, and she wanted Andrew to get over his fear of horses so the family could ride together.

"I guess." He sighed and brushed a lock of straight brown hair back from his eyes.

"Did you bring a helmet?"

"Uh-huh." Andrew stopped brushing Bandit and looked up at DJ. "Do I have to?"

"Yup. This is the day. We've put it off long enough, and I think you're ready. Everything should go great. Remember how well it went when you sat on him?"

"I guess."

DJ forced herself to keep a smile on her face and make the boy do what he'd agreed to. "Okay then, let me see you tack him up." She stroked the pony's nose to keep him calm. If Bandit so much as twitched right now, Andrew might head for the hills of Briones.

Andrew set the pad in place and looked up to see DJ's nod. He turned to take the saddle down—and stopped, taking in a deep breath and letting out a sigh that tugged at her heart. While DJ couldn't understand how a kid could be afraid of a horse, she also couldn't understand a mother forcing her child to do something he so obviously disliked. What if her own mother had made her take dance lessons, in a tutu no less?

"You're doing great."

Andrew nodded and set the saddle in place. Keeping a wary eye on Bandit's back feet, he reached under the pony's belly for the girth and buckled it.

"Okay, now check to make sure it's tight enough." DJ waited for Andrew to slide his fingers behind the webbing before doing the same. "Never hurts to double-check."

Andrew unlatched the halter and slid it off Bandit's nose, then reattached it around the pony's neck. All the time he slipped the bit into place and the headstall over the ears, he looked strung as tightly as a new wire fence. When he was finished, he turned to DJ.

"Okay, get your helmet." DJ nodded to the brand-new

helmet lying in the corner. Andrew put it on and buckled it in place. He didn't say a word, but his eyes accused her of child abuse.

"Very good. Now, let's lead Bandit out to the arena, just like you did before." DJ snagged a lead shank off the wall when they passed the tack room. She looked around, hoping against hope that Andrew's mother hadn't stayed to watch. Bridget had counseled against it, but the unease persisted. Mrs. Johnson so wanted to see her son riding.

They led Bandit around the arena once, then stopped by the fence, keeping a careful distance from the other riders.

Andrew's Adam's apple bobbed up and down, and he chewed his bottom lip.

"We've gone through these motions before, but this time you will swing your leg over the saddle and sit down. Ready?"

He nodded.

"Okay, facing Bandit, put your left foot into the stirrup iron." She kept the lead shank steady and used her other hand to assist her student. "Now, grip the pommel with your left hand and the cantle with your right, and pull yourself up. Use your leg muscles."

Andrew did as she said and, with her assistance at the last moment, swung his right leg over the saddle and sat down. The look he gave her tightened her throat. A grin tickled the corner of his mouth, and his eyes brightened.

"I did it."

"You sure did." She patted his knee. It was only with superwoman strength that she kept herself from hugging him.

"I did it all myself." Andrew kept one hand on the pommel, using the other to stroke Bandit's neck.

"Let's make sure your stirrups are the right length." She stepped to the front to see that they were even. "Good. Now

I'm going to lead you around the arena while you take up the reins and just hold them." She handed him the leather reins and rechecked his feet in the stirrups. "Ready?"

At his nod, she stepped out, Bandit moving gently beside her.

"S-s-stop."

They did. "Good boy," she whispered to the pony and gave him an extra stroke. "What's up?"

"I-I'm scared."

"Okay. Are your feet in the stirrups?" Andrew nodded. "And your seat is in the saddle?"

"Yeah, 'course."

"So you didn't fall off?"

"DJ, I'm sitting here, aren't I?"

"So what's there to be afraid of?"

"I might fall off."

"I'll make sure that doesn't happen, okay?" She checked the reins again and settled his feet back into the stirrups. "Ready?"

"I guess."

She led the pony halfway around the arena before stopping him. "How you doing?"

"Are we done?"

"Soon. You're doing fine."

"Hey, Andrew, way to go!" Tony Andrada waved and called from across the ring.

Andrew waved back. The smile got wider.

DJ could have danced around the arena. She even felt like shaking Tony's hand. By the time they'd circled the ring twice more, other riders had stopped to congratulate the little boy. Andrew wore a grin big enough to hold a wedge of watermelon. Joe and Bridget applauded from the rail.

"He will do fine from now on, ma petite," Bridget said after DJ had given the boy back to his beaming mother. "You have done a good job with him."

"I didn't think I'd ever get him on that pony." DJ shook her head. "And now I'm so proud of him, I could bust."

"That is the mark of a true teacher—one who receives as much of a thrill from watching a student master something as from doing it oneself."

DJ clutched the compliments to her heart.

That evening over at Joe and Gran's, Joe and DJ shared every detail of the afternoon with Gran.

"It was awesome," DJ said with a sigh and a shake of her head. "Hard to believe." She cocked her head to one side. "But you know, GJ, I still have one major problem."

Joe turned from where he was rinsing the dishes to put in the dishwasher. "What's that, darlin'?"

"Well, you're a guy, right?"

"I certainly hope so." Gran's chuckle made DJ smile.

"You know that's not what I meant, but . . ." She sighed. "I drew Tony's name for the gift exchange at the academy Christmas party."

"So?" Joe leaned against the counter and wiped his hands on a dishtowel.

"So I haven't a clue what to get him."

"What's the spending limit?"

"Five dollars. And I don't have that either, but since I already have to take money out of my saddle fund for Christmas, I guess that's that. But what do I buy him?"

Gran leaned back in her chair. "I think you ought to give him a drawing of his horse. That would please anyone. You have to admit, he does love his horse."

"You really think I should?"

"Why not? You draw wonderfully well."

"Yeah, but . . ."

"I'll help you with a frame. I know someone else who

would be really pleased to have one of your pictures—Robert. He'd take ours off the wall if we'd let him. Even though you're not really his daughter yet, he already brags about your accomplishments at work."

"He does? Wow."

Gran nodded. "And you know that story you were telling Bobby and Billy last time they were here?"

DJ propped her elbows on the table. "I was making it up as I went along."

"I was thinking you could write that down and do the drawings for it. They'd love it." Gran leaned forward and patted DJ's hand. "You have so much talent, darlin', and you have no idea."

"I have an idea I'm going to be totally swamped between now and Christmas. My term paper is due before vacation starts, too." DJ sent her grandmother a pleading look. "You think I could skip school till then?"

"Don't even think about it."

The next afternoon, DJ ambled over to Tony's stall and looked more closely at his horse. The Thoroughbred stood and watched her, his head over the web gate, tossing his head now and again in a way that made his forelock bounce. The white blaze was distinctive, like a star between his eyes with a long string down to a diamond-shaped patch of white between his nostrils. A blood bay, he had two white socks, and a white stocking that came clear to his knee.

As DJ studied the bay, she worked out the other details. Should she draw him in the stall or in the ring? She finally settled on a head sketch since her time was so limited. Anyway, drawing Tony in the saddle would be too hard. She still had a tough time getting the proportions right on people.

When she heard Tony's voice in the tack room, she scuttled back over to her own side of the barn. Her fingers were itching to take pencil in hand and begin drawing the lines that would bring the horse to life.

That night at home when the phone rang, she kept on sketching, leaving it for her mother to answer. Lindy came into the family room where DJ sat curled in Gran's wing chair.

"It's your father. He would like to come over again on Sunday."

DJ looked up, pulling her thoughts together. "Why?"

"He wants to see you again."

"Oh." DJ shook her head. "I can't Sunday. I plan to ride awhile and then we're going to decorate the tree. Robert and the Bs are coming, remember?"

"Guess we'll just have to do that in the evening."

"Why don't you tell him we've got other plans? That's what you tell me to say." DJ picked up her gum eraser and gently took out a couple of stray lines.

Lindy stood in the doorway a moment longer before returning to the kitchen. "That will be fine, Brad. We'll see you about two."

"M-o-t-h-e-r!" DJ catapulted out of the chair. Lindy was just hanging up the phone when her daughter hit the kitchen. "That's no fair! I need to ride, and the weather report said we are supposed to have a nice weekend. I haven't been up in Briones forever."

"Sorry. That was the only time he could come, and he's bringing you something."

"Fine, he can drop it off and leave."

"Darla Jean." The note of warning was lost on DJ.

"How come you guys make all the decisions, and I'm just supposed to smile and agree?" She stomped across the floor to the fridge. "I'm so far behind with everything already, I'll never catch up. . . ." She caught herself. Whoa, not the time to bring that up.

"Then it's a good thing you won't be taking time to go riding, isn't it?" Icicles dripped from the tone.

"You're not being fair. I'll go riding anyway."

"Darla Jean Randall, I think that is quite enough."

DJ clamped her mouth shut, grabbed her soda, and just managed to keep from slamming the refrigerator door. "If anyone else calls with plans for me, I'll be in my room." The only bad thing about carpeted stairs was that she couldn't stomp loudly enough, but DJ gave it a good effort. She knew better than to slam her bedroom door, however.

When she looked at the drawing in her hand, she shook her head and ripped the page off the tablet. Why would Tony want one of her lousy drawings, anyway?

At the party Saturday night, that same question troubled DJ. When it was Tony's turn to open his gift, she squeezed her eyes shut and clutched Joe's arm. What if Tony hated the picture?

11

"HEY, LOOK AT THIS." Tony held up the framed drawing for everyone to see. "Thanks, DJ." He looked at the illustration again and then at her. "Did you draw this?"

She nodded.

"Cool, it looks just like him. I didn't know you were an artist."

"Most people don't," Joe muttered, just loud enough for DJ's and Amy's ears.

"They will now." Amy poked DJ with her elbow. "You want money? Tell people you'll draw their horses—for a fee, of course. Hey, I'm a poet, too!"

"And you're a pain in the neck, but I don't go around telling everybody."

Tony passed the picture around amid oohs and ahs and "Wow, do you think you could do one for me?"

"How much would you charge, DJ?" Angie Lincoln's mother asked.

"I don't know."

Amy leaned around DJ. "She'll talk it over with her business agent and get back to you."

"Who?" DJ sent Amy a glare fit to fell a tree.

"Your business agent—me, of course. You've been getting me in trouble for years with your money-making schemes, and now I'm going to make sure you earn enough money that I don't ever have to do a pony party or raise hamsters again," she ended on a triumphant note.

Joe nearly fell off his chair laughing. Gran pushed him upright and winked at DJ. "See, darlin', I always told you your drawing would be a hit." She turned to her husband. "What's so funny?"

"Wish I had been in on the hamster hullabaloo. Knowing how much you like small, furry critters, that must have been a hoot."

"Mom's worse." DJ grinned at her grandmother. "You can bet they didn't try to help with the hamster roundup. And when John's friend volunteered to bring his boa constrictor over to hunt for his dinner, they really freaked. Mom yelled that hamsters in the garage was bad enough, but she would *not* permit a monster snake, too."

"I saw her freak at a garter snake once. 'Bout scared me half to death," Amy joined in.

"Who, Gran or Mom?"

"Your Mom. Gran can handle garter snakes."

"Thank you, Amy Yamamoto, you just made my day." Gran's smile could melt a block of ice at six paces.

"Attention, please." Bridget, list in hand, stood at the front of the room next to a table of trophies. "We have now come to the most important part of the meeting—the annual awards. Keep in mind that while not all awards are the Olympic gold, every person here deserves an award for his or her conscientious work, dedication to riding and improvement, and contributions to life here at Briones Riding Academy. I want to thank you all. That said, remember that many of *our* awards are of a different sort."

Applause broke out and died again.

"We will commence with the youngest and work our way up." Groans greeted the announcement. "You can wait your turn." Bridget's smile brought forth grins and squirming. "Emily Guerrero, please step up."

A five-year-old with dark hair and sparkling eyes got up from her place on the floor with the other little kids and came forward.

Bridget squatted down to be at Emily's eye level. "You might be our youngest rider, but, Emily, you are all heart." She pinned a heart-shaped badge that read *All Heart* on Emily's chest.

Applause and whooping continued as the younger kids paraded up for their awards. A hush fell when Andrew's name was called.

"Andrew, for your courage in overcoming your fear of horses, I crown you, Chief Courage." She placed a gold paper crown on his head that said *chief* and handed him a box of Lifesavers. "Whenever you need more courage, just think of your crown and eat one of these."

DJ shared a wet-eyed look with Gran. Amy nudged her and grinned.

"Thanks to you," Amy whispered.

Angie received a ribbon-tied fly swatter to chase yellow jackets, Amy got the golden hoof pick for her ability to pick even the dirtiest hoof clean, and David the beribboned pitchfork for cleaning stalls. The cheerleader-of-the-year pompon went to a blushing Tony for his most improved attitude.

"And DJ," Bridget beckoned.

DJ scrunched her eyes closed for a moment, wishing she could hide behind Joe. *What will she give me?* She stood and went forward in spite of her dread. She hated being in the spotlight like this—they could turn off the lights and her red face would make the room light as day.

"This award is not presented very often," Bridget smiled at the kids on the floor, "because we try hard here at the Academy not to make a practice of flying through the air—unless it is on the back of a horse. DJ, you have the honor of receiving a seat belt for your saddle. I crown you Queen of the Dumped."

DJ tried hard not to laugh, but she had to join in as Bridget placed a ribbon around DJ's neck with a gold-foil medal proclaiming her new title. The heat blazing on her face made her long for a fan as she fingered the medal on the way back to her seat. Someday she'd wear a real gold medal, and it wouldn't be a joke. Perhaps it was a good thing her mom and Robert had to go to his company party and miss this crazy award.

"And last, but not least, we have an award for Joe Crowder." Bridget held up a coffee mug with a rickety cartoon horse on it. "For the oldest new rider here."

After Joe returned to his seat, Hilary stood. "And now it's our turn." She carried a package to the front. "Bridget, for all your hard work and effort on our behalf, we give you this with our thanks and appreciation."

Bridget took the slender box and carefully slit the paper ends.

"Just rip it!" yelled one of the little boys.

Bridget winked at him and slit open the taped seam. When the box opened, she drew out a gift certificate, along with a picture. "A new sign for the pickup." She held up the artwork featuring the academy logo in blue, circled by the name and address. The phone number was at the bottom. "How perfect. Thank you."

"You have to take the truck into a shop to be painted," Emily informed her.

"Thank you," Bridget replied.

"We all gave money," Emily continued, until someone put a hand over her mouth and whispered in her ear. "But I was just—"

"And with that, won't you all come and help yourselves to dessert," Bridget said above the laughter.

Several people stopped DJ and commented on the picture she'd drawn. Before she realized it, she had promised to do several, but making sure they knew it would have to wait until after Christmas.

"Told you so," Amy whispered on her way back from a refill at the punch bowl.

"If you're so smart, why didn't you have a price list drawn up?" DJ hissed back. She turned to field another interested parent.

"I really don't do people very well—"

"Don't believe her, you can recognize her riders, too."

DJ felt like clamping a hand over Amy's mouth like someone had with Emily.

On the way home, she and Gran discussed fees and more about the drawing commissions.

"The fee should depend on the size of the picture." Joe swung the truck into DJ's driveway.

"Wonder how the company party is going for Robert? Shame he and your mother couldn't have been in two places at once. They'd have been proud of you."

"Oh, sure—Queen of the Dumped." DJ fingered the medal she still wore. "Did you see the look on Andrew's face tonight? And to see him up on that pony the other day—that was primo."

"You could come over to our house." Gran reached up to give DJ a half-hug over the seat.

"I know, but I need to work on some stuff here. If only the Atwoods weren't coming tomorrow, Joe, we could go riding. Look." She pointed at the star-filled sky. "Clear and supposed to stay that way."

"There'll be another day. We'll wait till you get in." Joe gave her a pat on the shoulder. "Good night, kid."

DJ worked on the book for the twins until her eyes refused to stay open any longer. When she turned off the lights and snuggled down under the covers, the medal she dreamed of gleamed with the luster of real Olympic gold.

The sunny morning, just cold enough so DJ could see her breath, did nothing for her sense of humor. If she skipped church, she could go riding. Maybe if she dawdled long enough over caring for Major, she would have an excuse. She *could* say she overslept. How would her mother know? Lindy had still been asleep when DJ left the house.

She propped her bike against the barn wall and trotted down the aisle and outside to Major's stall. Her whistle set half the barn to nickering, but Major outdid the others. He tossed his head, his forelock covering one eye. When she got close enough, he sniffed her pockets, finally finding his treat in the pouch of her hooded gray sweat shirt.

"Think you're pretty clever, don't you?" DJ teased as she dug out his carrot.

"He'd take your sweat shirt apart if you didn't give in." Joe stopped the wheelbarrow by Ranger's stall and began forking out dirty shavings.

"What would you say to going for a ride?" DJ let Major lean his forehead against her chest so she could rub the tips of his ears.

"Nice try, kid, but you know the rules."

DJ gazed up at the hills in Briones State Park. This would be such a perfect riding day. "We could hurry and be back in time for church."

"Washed and dressed by nine-thirty?" He looked at his watch. "Give me a break."

DJ muttered her way through feeding and stall cleaning. She gave Major a halfhearted grooming and dumped her gear back into the bucket. Why did grown-ups always have to mess up kids' lives?

When she got home, her mother was vacuuming the

family room. From the looks of her outfit, she planned on doing some major cleaning.

"Aren't you going to church?" DJ asked.

"Not if we're going to be ready for company all afternoon. You and Joe are picking up the tree on the way home. Your father is supposed to be here about two, and Robert will come out with the boys at four. Now, tell me when I have time to go to church."

"I could stay home and help you." *And go riding when we're done.*

"No, one of us better get some religion today, just in case it helps to keep the peace around here."

DJ headed for the kitchen to get some breakfast. When her mother was in *this* kind of mood, disappearing was the smartest move. And besides, if she couldn't go riding, she wasn't about to stay home and do housework.

While she dressed, DJ let her mind roam to Christmases past. Up until last year, it had been only the three of them—Gran, Mom, and her. Simple. They had decorated the tree the Sunday before Christmas, attended the midnight service on Christmas Eve, and opened presents on Christmas morning. Of course, Gran had baked lots of goodies, and DJ had helped when she could. But *this* year Gran was married and living in a different house, they had family all over the country, and suddenly DJ had a father.

She jerked the brush through her hair and made a face at the one in the mirror. Wrapping a scrunchy around her ponytail, she headed back to her room. The roar of the vacuum came up from downstairs. With a flinch, she returned to the bathroom, put the towels in the hamper, wiped out the sink, and hung new towels. A last-minute check told her the room passed muster and she wouldn't get yelled at. If she ever wanted to ride again, keeping on her mother's good side was a smart move.

She was just heading for her bedroom when she heard

the car honk—Gran and Joe were there. No time to make the bed or pick up the clothes strewn on the floor. She quickly closed the door, promising herself she would do it first thing when she got home.

DJ tried to stay tuned during the service, but she was only partly successful. When the choir sang "Prepare Ye the Way of the Lord," all she could think of was not being ready for Christmas. Would she have her presents completed in time? Her unfinished term paper was due Tuesday, the last day before vacation.

The pastor's sermon was on helping those less fortunate. DJ grimaced as she thought about what she'd done to help needy people this Christmas: nothing. When a special offering plate was passed to buy food baskets for poor families, she dug into her pocket and hauled out the ten dollars she had left for her Christmas shopping and dropped it in. Monday she'd have to go back to the bank, but knowing she'd contributed even that much made her feel better.

The light went on in DJ's head as the pastor went on to relay a story about a boy who gave coupons for lawn-mowing. She could do something like that! The rest of the service flashed by in a nanosecond.

On the way home, she kept thinking. What could she put in coupon booklets for her mom and Gran?

"See you guys later." DJ waved as Gran and Joe drove off. She trotted into the house, only to hear the vacuum running upstairs. Visions of her messy room made her close her eyes. So much for good intentions.

"Darla Jean Randall, it doesn't seem to me to be too much to ask that you keep your room reasonably neat. Look at that pigpen."

"You tell me never to go into your room without an invitation; why did you go into mine?" DJ wished she could snag the words back as soon as she said them. *Why can't I learn to keep my mouth shut?*

"I thought I'd do you a favor and vacuum for you." Lindy brushed her hair back behind her ears. "But not now. You know how I feel about messes, and they'll all be here before you know it."

"I'll get right to it," DJ promised through clenched teeth. Why was her mother so upset about company coming? It was just the usual crowd—plus Bradley and Jacquelyn Atwood. *That's what's bugging her*. "Would have saved a lot of hassle if you'd have just let me go riding this afternoon."

"That's the thanks I get." Lindy snapped off the vacuum and trundled it to the closet. "You can do the dusting when you get done with your room."

"As if I don't have enough to do." DJ yanked the covers up and jerked the comforter into place on her bed. With the stuff on her desk crammed in the drawer and her clothes in the hamper, the place looked pretty good. Of course, she hadn't vacuumed, but then . . . "Who cares." DJ clomped down the stairs to begin her dusting, well aware of how noises like stomping feet irritated her mother.

By the time the Atwoods arrived, the house was immaculate, Lindy wore an indelible white line around her mouth, and DJ's jaw ached from clenching it. When the doorbell rang, DJ had to force a polite smile on her face before opening the door.

Her father stood there with a huge box wrapped in shiny green paper and a big matching bow. "Merry Christmas, DJ."

Beside him stood Jacquelyn, her arms filled with a decorated basket filled with all sorts of odd-shaped things. “From me, too.”

“Merry Christmas . . . please come in.”

She eyed her father, half hidden behind his gift. What in the world could be big enough to need a box like that?

12

"IF YOU SHOW US TO YOUR TREE, we'll just put these under it."

"Uh, we don't have it up yet. We're doing that tonight, though this afternoon would have been better." DJ wished she hadn't added that last bit. Even to her ears, she sounded like a grinch.

"How are you, DJ?" Jacquelyn asked. "All ready for vacation?"

DJ led them into the family room. "No, I have to finish a term paper first." *How come they brought presents? We don't have anything for them. I never even thought of such a thing*. As her thoughts screamed in her head, she politely motioned them to seats and sat down in the wing chair, where she could face them.

"Sorry to be late." Lindy came down the stairs, her cream silk blouse and matching slacks set off by an emerald braided belt and emerald green earrings. She looked poised and relaxed—nothing like a few minutes before. "Coffee will be ready in a minute. Oh, what lovely gifts! How about if we put them over there for now?" She pointed to a spot by the wall at the end of the sofa.

DJ felt a giggle coming on. Her mother was incredible. DJ fingered her jeans—at least they were clean. And anything went with them, including her T-shirt, which showed a horse and said, *I'd rather be riding*.

"DJ, I brought pictures of our farm, some of the horses, and a few shows. Thought you might enjoy them." Jacquelyn patted the sofa between the two of them. "I'll explain who's who."

DJ joined them and, with the book spread out on her lap, got a glimpse of a life she'd never even dreamed of. The farm looked like something out of a magazine—all white fences, green pastures along a river bottom, and white buildings shaded by huge oak trees. While Arabs had never been her favorite breed, her father sure owned some beauties.

"That's Matadorian," Brad said, pointing to an obviously professionally done photo, "by Matador. Mares come from around the country to be bred by him. He's been national champion three times, and his get, or his offspring, take trophies wherever they go." Her father's pride was evident.

"He's a beauty."

"And smart." Jacquelyn shook her head. "You don't have to teach him something more than once. I wish my Hanovarian learned as quickly." They showed her photos of futurity shows and of dressage events.

"No jumpers?" DJ asked when she closed the book.

"Nope. It's never been an interest for either of us. That might have to change, though." His friendly smile made her think he planned to be around a lot. All these years of no one but Gran cheering her on, and now look at all the people on her cheering squad. That would mean butterflies at shows, big time.

"DJ, would you bring the plate of cookies?" Lindy asked as she entered with steaming cups of coffee on a silver tray. A glass of soda took up one corner.

"You don't drink coffee?" Brad asked DJ.

"She's only fourteen," Jacquelyn and Lindy said at the same time. They smiled at each other with a look that said, *Men!*

"Sorry, guess I forget. Seems I always drank coffee."

"You did, but I felt DJ needed to grow up before getting hooked on the stuff." Lindy set the tray on the coffee table. "DJ, the cookies."

DJ had been watching the exchange. She hadn't wanted to drink the bitter stuff yet—it had nothing to do with Lindy saying no. At another look from her mother, she headed for the kitchen, hurrying so she wouldn't miss anything.

After Brad had finished his coffee, he held the cup between his hands and stared at it a moment. "I have a favor to ask."

"Oh." Lindy settled deeper into the wing chair.

"Jackie and I would really love to have DJ come spend a couple of days with us during her Christmas vacation." He turned to include DJ in his range of vision. "If you want to, that is. I thought maybe you could bring a friend, if you'd like. I'd come pick you up and bring you back. I—*we* would so appreciate the time with you."

DJ glanced at her mother. Lindy's mouth wore faint traces of the white line again.

The silence that fell on the room made DJ itch.

"How about if DJ and I discuss this and get back to you?" Lindy crossed her knees and tented her fingers. "We'll let you know in the next day or so?"

Do I want to visit, or do I want to stay? I won't go without Amy . . . it would be exciting to see their place. The thoughts chased each other through DJ's mind like kittens skidding down a waxed hall.

"One other thing, we are leaving tomorrow to visit Jackie's family for Christmas, so if we've already left, just leave a message on the answering machine. I'll check in and get back to you right away."

"Fine."

DJ could tell Lindy's answer meant anything but.

They visited a bit more, then Brad patted DJ on the shoulder. "Well, we better be going. If what's in that box isn't to your liking, we can always exchange it." He got to his feet. "Thank you, Lindy, for the coffee and dessert. Hope you have a merry Christmas."

Jackie stood beside him. "Lindy, I do hope you will be willing to share your daughter with us. We promise to take good care of her. She's a fine young woman—one you can be proud of."

DJ felt the heat flame in her face. Why did grown-ups sometimes talk about you as if you weren't even there? As soon as all the good-byes were said and the door closed, she headed for the kitchen and the phone.

"Who are you calling?" Lindy leaned against the doorjamb.

"Amy, to see if she wants to visit them with me."

"I haven't said you were going yet."

At the tone of her mother's voice, DJ set the receiver back in the cradle. "Oh."

"Do you want to go? I thought you'd spend all your time riding, and you do have obligations at the Academy."

"I guess I want to go, if Amy can go along. Besides, I don't give lessons during vacation—Bridget knows working students are gone sometimes during holidays. All we have to do is let her know first." DJ stared at her mother. "You don't want me to go, do you?"

Lindy sighed and shook her head. "I don't know. Yes and no."

The doorbell rang and Robert's voice could be heard, calming the twins.

"We'll talk more later. Don't say anything yet, okay?"

DJ scrunched her face in a questioning look and shrugged. "Guess so. I better get the Bs before they batter the door down." She flung open the door to be bombarded with two high-power torpedoes. "Hi, guys."

"DJ, we was missing you! Christmas is almost here. You got any toys?" The two ran their sentences together as usual.

"I missed you, too. But sorry, no toys."

"How come? Gran has toys." Each of them had grabbed on to a leg and sat on a shoe, waiting for DJ to try to walk. With grins that split their cheeks, the Double Bs looked up at her with puppy-dog devotion.

DJ gave them their ride into the family room and collapsed on the floor, puffing as if she'd run a mile. "You guys get any bigger, and all rides are off." She let her arms fall to the sides and her tongue hang out.

One of the boys knelt next to her ribs and stared down into her eyes. "You okay, DJ?"

"No, I'm dying, can't you tell?" She let out a resounding groan.

The little one lay his head on her chest and an arm across her ribs. "Don't die, DJ. I likes you." The other one followed suit from the other side. "You our sister."

DJ wrapped her arms around both boys. "You two are the best brothers I ever had." She hugged them, then her hand crept into tickle position. Two jabs and they were writhing around, giggles exploding like firecrackers.

"I can tell you found DJ." Robert stood above the squirming pile and caught DJ's eye. "You need a break?"

"DJ likes us." More giggles and guffaws.

"I can tell." He turned at the sound of the doorbell. "Any time you've had enough, DJ, you let them know."

When the boys heard Grandpa Joe, they bailed off DJ and headed for the door.

Robert gave DJ a hand and pulled her to her feet. "I hear

you received a very special award at the party."

DJ groaned. "Does the whole world have to know about my getting Queen of the Dumped?"

Robert ruffled her hair. "Nope, just family." He dropped an arm over her shoulders. "Sorry we couldn't be there. Next year you can bet I'll check everyone's calendar before I schedule the company party."

DJ moved just a bit closer, and he tightened his arm. His hug felt good—nearly as good as one from GJ. She looked up in time to catch a sheen on Robert's eye.

"I've never had a daughter before, and now I'm about to have one who's nearly full grown. You've got a special place in my heart, kiddo, and don't you forget it." He hugged her again.

"Should I bring down the boxes of decorations?" Joe asked, lifting each twin-clad foot with difficulty.

"I'll help." Robert grabbed Bobby and Billy, tucked a boy under each arm, and crossed to dump them giggling on the sofa. "You two get out a book and read. Or go help Lindy set the table."

"Are we putting the tree in the living room where it's always been?" Gran asked after dropping her parcels in the kitchen.

"Where else?" DJ looked at her as though she'd wrapped her mind in one of the boxes.

"Well, it would look good in the corner of the family room where my painting mess used to be." She looked over at DJ when she didn't answer. "What is it, darlin'?"

"I miss your painting things, and I never thought they were a mess. This room just hasn't looked right since you left."

"Mel, you going to help us find things, or you just want us bulling around up there?" Joe called from the top of the stairs.

"I'm coming." Gran hurried after the two men. "Can't

have you rearranging the attic on such short notice, or we'll never find anything again."

DJ rubbed a sore spot on her chin with one finger. Oh, sure, a new zit. She studied the corner. The tree really would look nice there. "Come on, guys, you can help me to move stuff." Together, they lugged the magazine rack to the living room, temporarily moved the plants to the dining room until they could find a better place, and shoved a chair over to the other wall.

"What are you doing?" Lindy asked.

"Putting the tree here." DJ laid a hand on the curly head beside her.

"But I already arranged the living room." Lindy rubbed the inside of her cheek with her tongue. "Hmmm . . . you know, the tree would work really well in here." She stopped DJ and pointed to a spot on the floor.

"Oh no." DJ slapped her head with her hands. "A dust bunny."

"Bunny, where's a bunny? I don't see no bunny." The boys hit the corner running.

Lindy threw an arm over DJ's shoulders. "Shall we tell them?"

DJ shook her head. "Nope, keep 'em looking. Besides, one of their knees picked up the dust bunny, so now we won't have to haul out the vacuum." Thoughts of the earlier fracas flitted through her mind.

"Whose present?" The boys had found the big box left by Brad.

"Mine."

"What is it?"

"How should I know? It's a Christmas present, sillies."

"Open it and find out."

"Not on your life, guys." Lindy swooped down and snagged the twins by the bands of their pants. "We don't open presents until Christmas morning. Come on into the kitchen, I think I hear a cookie calling you."

"One calling DJ, too?" They grabbed her hands and all trooped out to the kitchen.

By the time they had the tree decorated, dinner eaten, and the house put back together, DJ felt like she'd been run through a cement mixer. Life wasn't easy with a twin Velcroed to each hip. When they all trooped out the door, DJ headed upstairs to work on her term paper. This promised to be a long night. And she hadn't even gotten to call Amy yet.

Sometime later, on returning from the bathroom, she heard her mother talking on the phone. In spite of all the years of both Gran and her mother cautioning against the evils of eavesdropping, DJ paused outside the door.

From the conversation, she knew Robert was on the other end.

"I know that, but what if he petitions for custody? You know that could happen."

DJ's heart hit her hip bones.

13

CUSTODY! I'M NOT LEAVING HERE. No way. DJ leaned closer to the partially open door.

"I know she's level-headed, Robert, but you've read about all those cases in the newspaper. I just don't want to go through any legal battles. But most of all, I don't want to lose my daughter."

You won't, Mom, you won't. DJ chewed on the tip of her finger. She shouldn't have listened. *What can I do? God, do you see what's happening? Please help us*. She tiptoed back to her bedroom and noiselessly closed the door.

"I'm not going to visit them if that's what's going to happen." She paced to the window and back. "But is Mom worrying about something that's never going to happen? I need to talk to Gran and Joe." She sank down onto her bed and worried her bottom lip between her teeth as she gathered up her term paper. All she had left to do was to rewrite it in decent handwriting. How come every time she thought things were going smoothly again, something messed things up? Was that the way life always was?

That night DJ dreamed she was being chased—again. It

was the first time in a while now. She jerked awake, heart pounding, mouth dry. Who was the man chasing her? And why? She turned on the light and headed for the bathroom. Surely by the time she went back to bed, the nightmare would be gone.

But it wasn't. She ran and ran, trying to scream, but no sound would come. Dark behind her, a light far ahead—would she make it in time?

Her alarm saved her. She woke up feeling as though she'd hardly slept.

"You look like you've been zapped by the Death Star," Amy said as DJ threw her backpack in the Yamamotos' car.

"Thanks for nothing. I can't help getting a zit."

"Not the zit, silly, you've got huge bags under your eyes and notebook paper has more color than your skin. You sick?"

"I didn't think so, but now I'm not so sure. You stay up half the night working on a term paper and see how you feel."

"That's why I always do my stuff early. I turned it in Friday." Amy ducked when DJ swung at her.

"One more day, just one more day and no school for over two weeks. I can get through it." DJ leaned her head against the back of the seat. "Oh, I almost forgot. Brad—"

"Your father?"

"What other Brad do I know? Anyway, he invited me to spend a couple of days at his house over vacation and said I could bring a friend. You want to go?"

"Do *you* want to go?"

"I'm not sure. Mom's all upset." DJ went on to tell her friend about the scene the night before—and her mother's worries. "You'd think I was moving out tomorrow the way she carried on." They'd reached their locker, and the bell was about to ring. "I don't know, Ames, I just don't know."

"Well, I'll ask my mom if I can go, if you want. Sounds like a primo place."

"I wanted to at first—I mean, all their horses and Jacquelyn doing dressage—she said she'd show me stuff and that I could ride one of their horses." The warning bell rang. "See ya."

DJ had a tough time keeping her mind on the rivers of the world in geography class. What was her mother going to say?

But Lindy didn't mention the invitation at all that night. In fact, her mother hardly mentioned anything. She wore the green look of a migraine headache when she came in the door and headed to bed as fast as she could climb the stairs. When DJ offered to bring some soup, Lindy groaned and refused.

"Just leave me alone, and maybe I'll be human again by morning."

DJ spent the evening rewriting her paper and working on the book for the Double Bs. Gran had a meeting and wouldn't be home till after nine. She'd nearly talked with Joe about the whole mess while at the Academy, but they hadn't had enough uninterrupted time. Concentrating on what she had to do took every bit of willpower she owned and some borrowed besides. If only she could have gone to Gran's after riding.

She chewed on the end of her pencil. They were supposed to call Brad. If only that phone call from Mr. Bradley Atwood had never come—and if only she hadn't eavesdropped. She wished she could go riding up in Briones to forget everything. She looked up to see rain rivulets running down the window. Fat chance!

When Gran hadn't answered the phone by ten, DJ gave up. Her final message said, "I'll talk with you tomorrow. I'm crashing."

School let out at noon. DJ let out a whoop and danced all the way to Joe's truck. "I'm free, I'm free! Free at last."

Amy followed behind her, shaking her head at Joe's grin. "Don't blame me that she's gone freaky. I'm just her friend."

At the Academy, DJ worked Patches without incident, to the surprise of both her and the owner. Mrs. Johnson had stayed to watch how DJ handled the horse so she could learn to ride him better. But when it was time for Andrew's lesson, she went to sit in the car and read a book like she always did.

Andrew mounted Bandit with only slight hesitation, grinning at DJ's words of praise.

"You won't make him go fast so I fall off?" His question caught her by surprise.

"Why would I do that?"

"You went fast, and you fell off."

DJ shook her head. "Andrew, my boy, you get some of the screwiest ideas. Falling off isn't such a big deal. Patches dumped me because he had too much pep and he likes to do his own thing. But Bandit is not like Patches—Bandit has known how to behave for years. Patches is just learning. Don't worry, buddy, you aren't going to fall off today. Okay?"

"Promise?" He looked at her from under long lashes.

"Near as I can." DJ snapped a lunge line on to the pony's halter. "Now, are your legs in the right place? Back straight? Tuck in your elbows, hold your chin up, and you are ready to ride." She moved him into the proper position as she talked. "Now, today you get to see what making the pony move feels like. You turn him with the reins, kind of like riding a bike, and you make him walk by squeezing with your legs." She pulled first one rein and then the other, then pressed his legs against the sides of the horse. "So when I say turn right, you pull the . . ." She waited for his answer.

"Right rein. Not hard, though."

"That's right. And to go forward?"

"Squeeze my legs, but not hard."

"Right. We don't do anything hard here. Horses like a gentle touch." DJ led Bandit out to the arena, through a gentle mist. The air smelled clean and fresh. Oh, to be riding herself! And not around the arena.

She closed the gate and led the pony onward, giving Andrew right turn, left turn, stop, and go commands. Little by little, she could see him relaxing, and a smile begin to curve his lips. At the stop, she turned again to face him. "Now, see this lunge line?" She held up the coiled rope. "You are going to start going in a circle around me. While you do that, you'll give Bandit his orders just like I did you. Got that?"

The smile flickered, and Andrew gritted his teeth. "I . . . I guess so."

DJ stepped back three paces, letting out the line as she went. "Okay, make Bandit go."

Andrew gripped the reins and squeezed his legs. Bandit walked forward like he always had. The boy turned to DJ with a grin wide on his face. "He did it. I made him go."

By the end of the lesson, his smile was a permanent fixture.

So was DJ's.

She understood much more how Andrew felt when Bridget refused to let her use stirrups during her dressage lesson later. "You remember how Major stopped the other day?" Bridget asked.

"How could I forget?"

"Your seat is much better, so I am sure that will not happen again. Remember what I said—when you pushed down with your pelvis, you pushed his backbone down, and that stopped him. Now, you must continue to drive him forward with your seat and legs. You did not have enough leg before."

"I know, balance between hand, leg, and seat. It sounds so easy in the book."

"You are right, it does sound easy. But nothing of value is ever easy, and you will be a much better jumper because of your willingness to work at this."

So you've said. DJ kept the words to herself—Bridget didn't care much for smart answers. By the end of the hour, her thigh and calf muscles were screaming and her back ached horribly. She was sure she'd hear the words "more leg" in her dreams.

When they finished the lesson, DJ surprised herself by asking Bridget a question. "Do you know of a woman named Jacquelyn Atwood?"

"Sure, she is a fourth-level rider from up north—Santa Rosa, I believe. Why?"

"Nothing much. Is she good?"

"To ride at that level you have to be. She has a wonderful horse, too. I cannot remember the name of the farm, but I believe her husband breeds Arabs."

"Atwoods' Arabians."

"Yes, that is it. Why all this interest in a dressage rider? You thinking of going on?"

"Me? Give me a break!"

"Sorry I asked. Keep practicing, though, DJ. You are doing well." Bridget waved and trotted through the mist to the office.

DJ watched her go, then used her legs to put Major into forward motion. If Andrew could learn new skills, so could she.

"Can we go to your house first?" she asked Joe on the road out of the Academy.

"Of course. I'll drop Amy off, and we'll be on our way. Your mother know this is the plan?"

"I left her a message." Now that the fun of riding was over, the questions came hurtling back.

Once at their house, she told Gran and Joe about eavesdropping on Lindy's conversation, then slumped back into her chair. "I don't know what to do."

"You can't do anything at this point, except talk with your mother. The two of you need to come to some kind of agreement." Gran drew a casserole dish from the oven and set it on the ceramic trivet on the table. "Would you please get the salad out of the fridge?" she asked Joe.

DJ sniffed appreciatively. "You baked bread, too."

"DJ, darlin', how many times have I told you not to eavesdrop?" Gran rested her hands on DJ's shoulders. "You wouldn't have so much to stew about if you hadn't overheard that conversation."

"I know, but I couldn't help it." DJ flinched under Gran's steady grip. She knew the look of disappointment that must be in Gran's eyes. "Don't tell, please? I won't do it again." She drew lines on the tablecloth with her fork tines. "But how else am I supposed to know what's happening? No one tells me—they just go ahead and do stuff. It's my life they're messing with."

"I know it must seem that way." Gran sat down, took Joe's hand, and reached for DJ's. "Let's say grace."

"Dear heavenly Father," Joe prayed, "bless this food so

lovingly prepared for us. Thank you for the blessings you have given us, one of them sitting right across the table. You know what needs to be done for DJ and Lindy, and we thank you that you are working it all out in your good time. We thank you and praise you. Amen."

"Doesn't seem like He's working it all out. Just seems to be getting worse."

"Might look that way, but it's always darkest before the dawn." Gran held out her hand for DJ's plate. "That's where faith gets a chance to grow, in that dark before dawn. So let's just thank Him in advance for the answers and go on about our business." She looked up to catch DJ's eye and passed her plate back.

"I guess."

"God sees the whole picture, kid, not like us who get only glimpses." Joe took his filled plate back. "Oh, Mel, this smells like something right from heaven."

"We're lucky it doesn't smell like turpentine or oil paint." She glanced down at the multi-dotted painting smock she still wore. "I had wanted that painting done in time to dry for Christmas, but it doesn't look like I made it."

"What are you working on?" DJ forked chicken and noodles into her mouth.

"A surprise for Robert. Thought he might like it for his new house."

"So it's for mom, too?"

"Will be, after they are married. I don't like to give a mutual present when they aren't exactly mutual yet. A lot can happen between now and February."

DJ stopped chewing on the bread heel she'd just buttered. "You think they won't get married?"

"No, it's just a kind of a superstition I have." Gran gave Joe a quick glance. "I know, I know—Christians aren't supposed to be superstitious, but old training is hard to break.

My mother threw more salt over her shoulder than went in her soup. So I'll give Robert this painting, and Lindy something else. Then they can enjoy both gifts together."

"Gran, you blow me away."

"Oh, darlin', you and I both know our heavenly Father is first and foremost in my heart. And we'll all keep praying that He becomes so for Lindy, too."

They ate in silence until DJ said, "So . . . what do you think I should do about going to visit the Atwoods over Christmas break?"

"The Atwoods?" Gran arched one eyebrow.

"I don't know what to call him—them." DJ shook her head. "I hate making decisions."

Gran looked at DJ over the rim of her violet-banded coffee cup. "I think you need to go see him—if not right away, then soon. You have a right and a need to know your biological father if it's possible, and in this case, it certainly is. Between Brad and Robert, you are one mighty blessed girl to have two such fine men in your life."

"Three."

"Three?" The eyebrow went up again.

"GJ. I've got him, too."

"Funny you should say that." Gran patted Joe's hand. "And he even does dishes." The twinkle in her eyes brought an answering one from the man beside her.

"Flattery will get you everywhere. I suppose that was a hint so you could go back to painting?"

"Right."

"Good. You do that and DJ will help me with the dishes so we can make time to work on her frames. Right, kiddo?"

DJ groaned and made a face. "Think I like dishes?" But she began gathering the plates to take to the sink. "Maybe tomorrow you can help me with the Double Bs' book, huh, Gran?" She elbowed Joe away from the sink. "And if it's nice, Joe and I can ride up in Briones."

"More rain predicted."

"You sure know how to make me happy." Their banter continued as they rinsed dishes and stacked them in the dishwasher.

When her mother hadn't come by for her by ten, DJ climbed into bed in her bedroom at Gran's. At least this way she and Joe could get going early in the morning. As she closed her eyes, she thought a moment of the big box waiting at home. Whatever could be in it?

14

"I'LL NEVER GET THIS THING RIGHT!"

"Just ask that cute guy over there for help. That's why he works here." Amy looked up from the photocopy machine at the Copy House to grin at DJ. "You just have no patience."

"With horses, yes. Machines, no." DJ made her way past the busy machines, most manned by people using red or green paper to make Christmas letters, up to the desk.

"Hi, can I help you?"

Amy was right, he *was* cute, but right now DJ needed brains. "I can't get that machine to print on both sides. I think we're following the directions." DJ pointed to the machine that she was sure was sticking its tongue out at her.

"I'll be there in a minute, okay?"

"Sure, thanks." She felt like stomping back to the machine. Why did everything seem to go wrong when she was in a hurry? At this rate, the cards would never be printed, and DJ was anxious to get going as soon as Joe got back. Today they were finally heading for a ride in Briones.

Amy finished printing the backs of her cards and moved on to the paper cutter. The photos had turned out beautifully clear: one of a rose from her mother's garden, another of her little sister eating an ice cream cone, a view of fog over San Francisco Bay, and one of a goose swimming in a pond. Each packet would hold two of each card, for a total of eight.

DJ's horses probably wouldn't appeal to as many people, but she knew her family would be pleased. Bridget had said she'd carry them in the tack shop, too, so DJ was running off twenty sets.

The young man flipped a couple of buttons, checked on the card stock paper, slammed the machine closed again, and pushed the green button. Her page came out as clear as could be.

"Thanks."

"No problem." He held up the sheet of card stock. "Hey, that's really cool. Did you draw that?" At her nod, he studied the drawing of the foal again. "My sister would love something like this. She's nuts about horses. You making note cards?"

"Yeah, for Christmas presents." DJ stopped, caught the nod from Amy, and continued. "And we'll be selling them, too."

"Could you get me a set or two? How much are they?"

DJ stumbled over her tongue. On the second try, she answered, "There are eight to a pack, and the packs cost four dollars. My friend Amy has reproductions of her photos on hers." She pointed to the paper cutter table.

"Cool. Are the two of you in business or something?"

"Sorta."

He stopped for a minute, studying the growing stack of 4×5 ready-to-fold cards. "Could I buy two sets from each of you? Makes my shopping easy."

Amy looked up. "Sure, we'll package them and bring them back here tomorrow. If you've got any friends here who might like them, let them know we'll bring extras."

DJ rolled her lips together to contain a grin. *Leave it to Amy not to miss a trick.*

When the Copy House employee walked off to help someone else, the girls swapped high-fives. "That'll at least help pay for the envelopes." DJ removed her sheets from the machine and took over Amy's place at the cutting board. "If we sell enough, we'll have free Christmas presents to give. Why didn't we think of this a long time ago?"

Amy folded her cut cards. "You know, maybe we should charge five dollars instead. I checked at a stationery store, and note cards were priced all the way up to $7.95 for a package of ten."

"You know what my mom says, you've got to price stuff according to what the market will bear."

"Woowee, listen to the big business woman over here!"

As soon as they finished cutting the cards, they paid their bills and headed out to the truck where Joe waited.

"You can see if you promise not to tell anyone." DJ couldn't wait to show him.

"Promise."

Each girl handed Joe samples of her cards. A hush fell as they waited for his opinion.

"These are really good." He shuffled through them again. "I'm impressed. Are these Christmas gifts, or your latest money maker?"

"Both. We sold two packs each to a guy who works at the Copy House." DJ bounced on the seat in her excitement. "Now we can go riding. Hurry up, GJ, the horses are waiting." She and Amy took their cards back and carefully put them into their bags. No bent corners or smudge marks would do.

Amy gently tucked the package into the glove compartment. "Hey, I forgot to tell you. My mom said I could go to your father's farm with you, if you still want to go."

"That's the question, isn't it?" DJ slid her fingers up and down the seat belt crossed over her chest. She nodded. "Yeah, we'll go. I'll call him and make the final plans."

Joe patted her knee. "I'm proud of you, DJ. You'll make it."

DJ flashed him a grin. "Promise?"

"Promise."

While clouds crept over the hills as they saddled, DJ refused to give in. The three of them were going riding, and that was that. If they got sprinkled on, so be it. The wind picked up, and they could feel the temperature dropping as they rode up the hill and out of the Academy. Through one more gate, and they were on park land, hills now covered with the green of winter thanks to all the rain they'd had. One hillside had been so rain soaked it had given way and slid downward, leaving a bowl of exposed dirt and rumpled ridges of grass-covered dirt below. The cattle that had free range in the park ran before them as if they were being chased when they made their way down the path to the staging area, a parking lot for park visitors. During the busy park season, a ranger took fees in a small building at the entrance to the parking lot.

Since mountain-bike riders and hikers loved the trails as much as horse riders did, the park was always well used. Today, however, the parking lot was empty.

DJ nudged Major into a canter as they took the main trail under the trees and followed a creek that now held plenty of frothing water. In the summer it was only a trickle.

"Come on, GJ, doesn't that young pony of yours know how to enjoy a real ride?"

"Just watch and you'll see." Joe kept a careful hand on the reins.

Ranger whinnied as the other two horses disappeared around a curve.

"I love riding right before a storm," DJ shouted.

"Me too." Amy kept Josh at the same even gait as they climbed the well-kept fire road trail.

DJ glanced over her shoulder. "Hey, look who's catching up!" What fun it would be to really run, to race up the hill and across the meadow, to let Major have his head and just go.

Major snorted and tugged at the bit. He wanted the same thing.

DJ was tempted, but she kept the easy rocking-chair canter that ate up the miles. Not only was it easier on her horse, but it was safer should the trail be slippery. They rounded another corner, and she signaled a halt, this time with seat and legs instead of just pulling on the reins. Major obeyed instantly.

A washout had dug a three-foot wide and half as deep ditch across the trail. If they'd been galloping, they'd have had to jump over or stumble through it. Sloppy mud all around made footing treacherous.

DJ looked at Amy and shook her head. "Sure glad we weren't racing."

"Me too. That could have been a bad one."

Ranger stopped beside them, front feet dancing while he pulled at the bit and tossed his head. Joe leaned forward and, keeping one hand snug on the reins, stroked his mount's neck.

"Easy, fella." He looked around. "These hills must be soaked for the runoff to be this bad. You'd think that was a regular creek. Well, guy, guess you are going to get a lesson in crossing water. Lead on, DJ. Major will be cautious, but he'll go."

DJ squeezed her legs, and Major, placing his feet with utmost caution, negotiated the two-foot drop, splashed in the ankle-deep water, and headed up the other side. Josh followed suit, snorting all the way.

Ranger, however, would have none of it. He snorted and backed up fast. When Joe brought him up to the water again, he let the horse put his head down and sniff.

Major nickered, as if encouraging the younger animal.

Ranger put one foot forward, then the other. Joe talked to him gently, but when the gelding put his foot into the water, he sat back on his haunches and whirled around. Had Joe not kept a firm hand on the reins, Ranger would have headed for home.

"Easy, fella," Joe kept up the murmur as he dismounted. "Guess we'll do it this way. You'll have to learn someday. We should have made you go through water before—a good trail horse does all this stuff." Joe led him down and stopped at the edge of the running stream. "Now, you *could* just jump over this thing if you had a mind to, but we're going to walk it." He pulled on the reins.

Ranger snorted and he rolled his eyes. He moved to back up, but the steady hands on his reins and Joe's gentle voice kept him coming forward.

DJ watched the process, swapped concerned glances with Amy, and found herself praying, *God, please get that fool horse through this safely*.

Ranger splashed water with one foot and leaped forward. If Joe hadn't been prepared, he'd have been run right over. The gelding now stood trembling on the other side.

Joe patted him and told him how great he was.

DJ breathed a sigh of relief. "You know, you really should make him go back and forth a couple of times to get him comfortable with it."

"I know." Joe grinned up at her. "Want to trade horses?"

"Not me. Just think what this would be like with Patches. I know Mrs. Johnson wants to ride up here. Soon it'll be time for me to get him used to things like this."

Joe led Ranger back and forth across the stream, then mounted to cross a last time and head up the trail. Ranger snorted but stepped down and through the water as though he'd never thought of charging or refusing.

"Good boy," Joe said, stroking the horse's neck and grinning at DJ and Amy. "Well, we had our excitement for the day, wouldn't you say?"

"He's going to be a good horse," DJ said, a smile now chasing the worry away. "I thought maybe that was the end of our ride."

"Nah, I knew he'd do it."

"Just not when, right?" Amy patted Josh's neck. "I remember the first creek he crossed. He wasn't a happy camper."

When they crested the trail and reached the meadow, low clouds cottoned the hilltops and sent tendrils exploring the valleys. Off to the right, the river flowing through the Carquinez Straits lay molten gray. The smokestacks of the refineries in Martinez puffed steam clouds that plumed due east, and the trees above them whipped in the wind, small limbs and dead leaves scurrying before the onslaught.

The air hung heavy with the promise of rain.

DJ sucked in a deep breath and turned to grin at Amy. "Don't ya love it?"

"It's going to get wet out here pretty soon. Think we better turn back?" Joe stopped beside them.

"We should, but let's ride up to the saddle where the bluebird houses are. I hate to turn back."

When the others agreed, DJ nudged Major back into a canter and they followed the road around the curve and up the hill. Cattle grazed the slopes and watered at the pond that now looked like a small lake. She wanted to keep going, down into the valley and around the other hills. Even with all the riding she'd done in the park, she'd never followed all the trails. There was never enough time.

Reluctantly, DJ turned back. Soon, she promised herself. Soon she'd follow that trail around the north side of the hills, the one that didn't look as well used as the others.

They were drenched by the time they made their way back into the stable yard.

Back at Gran and Joe's after DJ had taken a shower to warm up, she and Joe finished the last of the framing and Gran helped her assemble the book for the twins.

"That's it then," DJ sighed when she tied the last bow on the packages. "My Christmas presents are finished."

"And none too soon, with Christmas Eve tomorrow night." Gran set a plate of cookies on the table. "Try these and see if we should make more of them. I made up a plate of goodies for you to take to the Yamamotos. You want to drop it off on your way home?"

"Sure." DJ grinned around a mouthful of cookie. "You better start mixing, Robert's gonna clean these out." She plucked a chocolate kiss off the top of the round peanut butter cookie. "How come we never made these before?"

"I didn't have the recipe before." Gran poured coffee for her and Joe and set a mug of hot chocolate in front of DJ. "You want a drop of coffee in that?"

"Mocha? You bet." DJ took a swallow. "Thanks, Gran, you're the best."

"After Christmas we'll have to invite Shawna to stay over." Joe leaned back in his chair. Shawna, who dreamed of taking riding lessons someday, was the only daughter of Joe's son Andy.

As he proceeded to impress Gran with tales of their ride, DJ felt locked on the words "after Christmas." After Christmas—next week to be exact—she would be going to her father's house for the first time. Three days away from Major, and three days with a man she hardly knew. Could she stand it?

15

HAVING LOTS OF RELATIVES sure made a difference at Christmastime.

Early in the afternoon, DJ gave Major his gift—extra horse cookies and a new halter. She gave Patches a treat and then went to see Bandit and Megs. The mare greeted her like a long-lost friend, making DJ feel guilty for not paying the retired jumper more attention since she got her own horse. She'd begun jumping lessons on Megs, Bridget's show horse of many years.

"See you tomorrow," she told Bandit. "You'll have plenty of kids to entertain." Bandit snuffled in DJ's pocket for more treats and was rewarded with a carrot piece. "You're too smart for your own good." She gave him an extra pat, and after making sure Major had fresh water and hay and had finished his grain, she trotted out to ride her bike home. Sun peeked through the patchy clouds, and while the weather announcers said storms were lining up out on the Pacific, tomorrow was supposed to be nice.

Since Amy and her family had already left for the weekend to visit her grandparents, DJ rode alone. Joe had offered her a ride, but as he and Gran were hosting everyone for dinner, she'd done his chores at the Academy, too. Tonight would be like Thanksgiving had been—one long slumber party.

"Hurry up or we'll be late," Lindy called from her bathroom as soon as DJ mounted the stairs.

"I'm hurrying." DJ draped her horsy jeans and shirt over the back of a chair. They weren't dirty, just full of horse hair and stuff. She'd wear them for chores in the morning. Honestly, if her mother had her way, the smell of horses would never pass the kitchen door. What was going to happen at their new house when the twins had ponies and she had Major? How would her mother stand it?

DJ climbed into the shower. Thoughts like that always gave her the shivers. Life had changed so much already, and as far as she could see, it was changing big time in the months ahead.

Her mother gave her a didn't-you-have-something-nicer-to-wear-than-that look when they met downstairs. DJ shrugged. Compared to her mother, she looked casual. But at least she wasn't wearing jeans and a T-shirt. She had on navy corduroy pants and a real shirt with buttons up the front. She'd even ironed it. If she could have found a belt, the outfit would have looked more put together, but she was running late. As usual, the look from her mother said.

DJ picked up the last box of presents and followed her mother out to the car. They'd already taken over most of the wrapped packages, including the big one from her father, the day before. Once in the car, DJ thought again about the big box. More than once, she'd been tempted to open it very carefully, peek in, and wrap it back up.

She glanced at her mother. What would she have done if she caught her daughter sneaking a peek at Christmas presents? DJ grinned. It wasn't worth the chance of being found out, so she'd left well enough alone. Whatever it was sure felt heavy when she shook it—accidentally, of course.

Every light in Gran and Joe's house was on, and the outside looked like a fairyland with small white lights around the windows, doors, trees, and along the roof peak. DJ had helped Joe and Robert put them up two weeks earlier.

"Isn't it lovely?" Lindy breathed. "Robert said next year we are going to do our house." She leaned on the steering wheel. "You know, we haven't put up outside lights since Grandpa died. Do you remember the way he used to decorate?"

DJ shook her head. "I was just a twerp, Mom. The only thing I remember was that the tree was always in the living room corner." She gathered the shopping bags and presents and opened the car door. Gran had carols playing on an outside speaker.

"O Holy Night, the stars are brightly shining . . ."

DJ looked up. The carol was right.

They were the last to arrive. Andy and Sonya with daughter, Shawna, greeted them in the doorway and led the way to stack the remaining presents under the tree, now nearly hidden by gaily wrapped packages.

After dinner at warp speed, the entire family trooped off to the Christmas Eve service. This year, they hadn't waited for the midnight service because of the younger children. They all accepted their white candle with its cardboard shield at the door, and with one twin on each side, DJ followed Robert into the pew. The church glowed with candlelight, and the organ swelled with the age-old carols.

DJ breathed in the scent of evergreens, shushed the boys, and closed her eyes for just a moment. This was her favorite service of the year. A hush fell as if the entire roomful of people stopped breathing at the same instant.

A violin sang the opening bars of "What Child Is This?" joined by a flute and finally the piano. Times like this, DJ wished she'd taken time to learn to play an instrument. She could feel the music tugging at her throat, making the backs of her eyes burn. The words crescendoed in her mind: "This, this is Christ the King . . ."

She put an arm around each of the twins and hugged them to her.

As the verses told the story of the Christ child's birth, she thought of the shepherds, smelled the hay in the stable, and imagined a cow lowing. It was easy to be there in her mind. Her fingers itched to draw the scene.

"Come, see where He lay," the pastor announced from the pulpit. "He came for you and for me, giving up all His godly powers—He who was at the beginning of creation. Think of it! He did this for you, for me, for all people. Think what it would be like if you left all your human qualities and took on being a grasshopper. He who brought us into being gave up being God—for us."

DJ leaned forward, elbows on her knees. Bobby and Billy did the same.

"He loves us that much."

She flashed a glance at her mother, sitting on the other side of Robert. Were those tears shimmering in her eyes? The burning behind her own eyes grew more insistent.

"No matter what we do, no matter how hard we try to run away, even when we try to ignore Him, He loves us."

At the end of the sermon, when everyone stood for the hymn, DJ felt like hugging everyone who stood around her. The choir sang during the offering, then the lights dimmed. The altar candles were extinguished, and the tree darkened.

The pastor walked down to stand directly in front of the congregation, a tall, thick candle in the hands of one of the teenagers beside him. "We read from the first chapter of the gospel of John, 'In the beginning was the Word, and the Word was with God, and the Word was God. He was with

God in the beginning. . . . In him was life, and that life was the light of men.' "

Two more teens came forward, lit their candles at the pastor's, and one by one the light moved down the center aisle and then out into the rows. "Silent night, holy night . . ." When each person had lit a candle, then he could begin singing.

The boys fidgeted beside DJ. When the candle came to their row, DJ watched as each member of her family lit a candle from the one beside. The Bs bounced in their excitement. Gran held her candle steady and the first twin dipped his, oohing at the light he now held. DJ lit hers, sharing her flame with the second twin, who shared his with Robert.

DJ felt an uneasy flutter in her stomach as the sea of flames around her grew. She took a deep breath. Both boys proudly held their candles up to her face to show her the flames. A fist seemed to grab her throat as hot wax dripped onto her hand. *Fire!* She felt the familiar fear take hold. Was someone screaming?

16

"DJ, YOU ALL RIGHT?"

"Please, DJ!"

The boys' cries sounded as if they were a mile away.

"I . . . I'm fine." DJ blinked and took a deep breath. Robert held her hands in his, and Gran wrapped her arm around her granddaughter's shoulders. "Wh-what h-happened?"

"The fire, darlin'. You know how the memories can affect you. I suppose all the candles . . ." Gran's whisper in her ear brought DJ back to the moment. What had she done? Gone all kooky again? How embarrassing.

DJ looked to see tears pooling in the big blue eyes of the Double Bs. "Hey, guys, you didn't do anything wrong. It's just me . . . and . . . and fire. We don't get along too well." She forced the words past the desert in her throat. All around them, people were extinguishing their candles as the lights came back up. The pastor gave the blessing, and the organ broke into "Joy to the World."

DJ stood with the rest of them. She rubbed the wax off her wrist and covered the scar in the middle of her palm with the other hand. *All because of a couple silly little candles. What kind of a weirdo am I?*

The boys glued themselves to her side, shooting her

anxious looks when they thought she wasn't looking. On the ride back to Gran's, the conversation flowed around her as though she were a rock in the middle of the stream. And like a rock, she had no voice—except inside her head, where several voices argued about how stupid she was. She rubbed the scar again as if the action would bring back the memory. One day she would have to ask Gran again how it had all happened.

"It's okay, darlin'," Gran said, pulling DJ close as they walked up the sidewalk to the house. The luminaries they'd made out of brown sacks with a candle and sand in them lit the way.

"I spoiled the service for everyone."

"No, no one around us even noticed."

"Was I screaming?"

"Of course not. Did you think you were?"

DJ nodded. "I heard someone screaming, but now that I think about it, it sounded like a little kid." She took a deep breath. "Well, that's over." She grabbed one of the twins by the back of his jacket. "First one into the house gets to turn on the tree!"

Later they hung all the stockings from the fireplace mantel and stood back to admire them.

"Santa's got a big job there," Robert said. "You think he's up to it?"

"Santa's going to bring me a pony," one of the twins announced.

"Me too." The other looked up at their father. "That's all I asked for."

Robert groaned. The other adults snickered.

"Okay, bedtime." Robert clapped his hands. "Santa can't come till you're asleep."

DJ debated whether to stay up longer, but the look in Shawna's eyes made her decide to hit the sack. She and Shawna were sharing the bed, and the boys had sleeping bags on the floor in the grandkids' room. She heard her mother leave with Andy and Sonya while Robert headed for the other guest room. Slowly the house settled down. She shushed the boys again, and Shawna giggled softly.

"Daddy!"

"What now?" Robert came to the door.

"I wanna drink of water."

"Me too."

Robert brought two plastic glasses. "Last time. I hear one more peep from you two, and no Santa."

More giggles. Quiet again.

"Tomorrow we get to ride," Shawna whispered. "I can't wait."

"You want to spend a couple of days of your Christmas vacation out here with me?"

"Really?"

"If it's okay with your mom," DJ whispered back.

"That would be the best Christmas present ever."

DJ fell asleep hearing the violin and flute soar with the notes of "What Child Is This?"

"DJ, wake up. It's Christmas!" Four small hands tugged at her blankets and patted her cheeks.

"Go 'way," she mumbled, scrunching her eyes closed.

"Come see the presents."

"Now, DJ." A giggle, then another.

DJ opened one eye. "It's still dark out. You can't get up till it's light." She covered her head with the quilt.

"We can *turn* on the lights."

"Nope. No Christmas till it's light outside. Hit the sack, guys."

"Go get Daddy," she heard one whisper.

"No, you don't. Let him sleep. Let *me* sleep—just till light."

Shawna smothered a giggle beside her.

DJ closed her eyes and tried to go back to sleep. All she could see was that big box. Today she'd find out what was in it! She could hear the boys turning over and over. They whispered about as quietly as a train whistled.

"Okay, fine—go get your poor daddy up."

They erupted from their sleeping bags with matching shrieks and streaked down the hall.

"Quietly," DJ sighed. "Come on, Shawna, we don't want to miss anything."

"No presents until everyone gets here," Robert decreed when he met her in the hall. "And until the adults get their first cup of coffee." He rubbed his eyes and winked at DJ. "Thanks for keeping them down for a little while longer."

"You heard?"

"Of course." He gave her a one-armed hug on his way to the kitchen, where the tempting smells of coffee and cinnamon rolls beckoned. Gran even had the table set already.

DJ sat cross-legged on the floor with the boys, who were eagerly digging in their stockings, spreading their treasures all around. Tiny packages were tightly bound with tape to slow their nimble fingers. When they reached the sock toes, each held up a shiny silver dollar.

Shawna and DJ joined the excitement and dug into their stockings. By the time DJ had unwrapped each small treasure, she had new drawing pencils, erasers, hair scrunchies, a booklet of coupons for the local hamburger place, gum, mints, a popcorn ball, a tangerine, and a pomegranate.

"What's that?" The boys abandoned their socks to come examine hers.

"A pomegranate."

"What do you do with it?"

"Eat the seeds. I'll show you later." She dug down to the toe of her stocking and retrieved her silver dollar.

"We gots those in our banks."

"Daddy said not to spend them—they special."

"You are, too." She ruffled their curls and set them to giggling with tickles. Her eye kept wandering back to the big box set to the back of the tree.

By the time everyone finally congregated in the living room, the boys were wound tighter than a twister.

"Shawna, you want to play Santa Claus?" Robert asked.

"I thought that was my job," Andy moaned.

"I get to help."

"Me too." The twins bounced in front of the tree.

"Okay, okay." Shawna sat by the tree, dug out the gifts, read the names, and handed the boxes to the boys to deliver. With everyone waiting to watch each person open a present, DJ could tell this would be a long process. Should she ask for the big box first? If only it hadn't been stashed behind the other presents!

Soon brightly colored paper and ribbons decorated the floor in spite of Gran's continual folding. Robert wore a wobbly smile when he thanked DJ for the framed drawing, and the note cards were a huge success. The pile of gifts beside DJ continued to grow. She'd never have to buy clothes again—or drawing paper.

It took both boys to carry the big box to her. She split the paper open with trembling fingers.

"Who's it from?" Bobby asked. DJ had pinned name tags on the twins earlier, saying, "I'm going to figure out who's who or bust."

"My . . ." What to call him? "My father." She glanced up to catch a frown streak across her mother's face.

"Hurry, DJ, I wanna see."

"So do I, guys, so back up!" She grinned and tickled the little boy to make him scoot back. Slowly she unfolded the flaps and got up on her knees to look into the box. Pushing aside the packing material, she stopped breathing. "Oh." Her breath came back on a sigh. "A saddle." She looked under the saddle leather for the brass nameplate. "A Crosby."

DJ lifted out the saddle, scattering foam peanuts in the action. She stroked the fine leather. Never had she dreamed of having such a fine saddle. She'd been saving for a used one. A Crosby all-purpose saddle, she could use this one for jumping, for dressage, and just riding. She looked up to see Robert and her mother exchange meaningful glances.

"There's more." Billy lifted out a new headstall.

Her father wouldn't have known she already had a new one, given to her by Angie's family after the beesting incident.

DJ opened the card attached to the stirrup. *I hope you can use this*, her father had written. *If you need something more, or if the saddle doesn't fit just right, we can always exchange it.*

"Sit in it, DJ!" a twin squeaked.

"No, can't do that unless it's on a horse, or you can break the tree."

"What tree?"

Joe saved her explaining. "Well, that is some surprise." He broke the silence that had fallen on the adults. "I know you'll get a lot of good use out of that. Shawna, there's another box for DJ behind the tree."

This one held a new blue blanket for Major. It even had his name sewn in the corner. The card read *With all our love, Gran and GJ*. DJ leaped from the floor and threw her arms around them both. "Thank you. You knew mine was pretty ratty."

Shawna came over and stroked DJ's new saddle. "Sure is pretty."

Robert and Andy slapped their knees and rose in sync.

"Far as I know, there's still one more present." Robert looked at Joe. "You ready, Dad? This is kind of a present from the whole family."

"I guess. What did you young pups get into now?" Joe got to his feet, ribbons and bits of paper slipping to the floor.

"Hmmm. How are we going to do this?" The two brothers grinned at each other.

"I say we blindfold the bunch and lead 'em out," Andy suggested. "Gran, you got any extra dish towels?"

"How many do you need?"

"Ummm . . ." Robert counted. "Joe, DJ, Shawna, the twins . . . five'll do it." As soon as all the blindfolds were in place, they led the staggering, giggling parade outside.

"Where are we going?" DJ blew the corner of her blindfold off her lips.

"You'll see. Step carefully now." Lindy had DJ's hand.

DJ shuffled her feet. How strange to be blinded like this. What was going on?

"Okay, what's up?" Joe asked ahead of her.

"You'll see."

"Hey, Billy, no peeking."

"Are you ready? Now, on three, you can all take off your blindfolds. One, two, three!"

DJ whipped the dish towel off her head and gasped.

"Well, I'll be!" Joe let out a roar. "You, you . . ."

DJ looked at Shawna with a grin.

"But I don't have a horse." Shawna looked to her father. A sudden grin lit her face like a megawatt candle. "But I get one, don't I?"

"As soon as we find one we all like."

She ran and threw herself into her father's arms.

DJ let herself be pulled forward till she stood next to the shiny silver four-horse trailer. A huge red ribbon was tied in a bow on top of the roof.

"Look at that. Dual wheels." Joe placed a hand on DJ's shoulder. "And a changing room."

DJ opened the door and peeked inside. Two tiny whirlwinds zipped around her and began exploring.

"How come for us?"

"'Cause we gets ponies!"

Shawna ducked under her arm. "DJ, I'm getting a horse—you heard him." The light still shone in her face.

"Who do we thank?" DJ turned to the rest of the family, all lined up watching and laughing at the new trailer owners.

"Check the card." Robert pointed to an envelope fastened to the ribbon streamer.

DJ opened it, and Joe read. "To our horse people, with love from Robert, Lindy, Andy, Sonya, and Gran."

"How did you manage to get this here without me noticing?" Joe asked.

"We'll never tell." Robert had his arm around Lindy's shoulder. "Besides, if Lindy and I get horses, we'll need a larger one."

DJ felt her jaw hit her chest and bounce back up to snap closed. Her mother? On a horse? That would be the day. She crossed to the group and, starting with her mom, gave them all hugs and thank-yous. What a day. What an incredible, four-star, awesome, wonderful day! A saddle *and* a horse trailer.

Bobby and Billy jumped on the tailgate and chased each other around the rig.

DJ looked at her mother. She could tell something was bothering her, even though she was laughing at something Robert had said. The tiny furrows between Lindy's eyebrows were a dead giveaway. Was it the saddle?

DJ chewed her lip. *I bet it is*, she thought, *I just bet it is. Now what's going to happen? She won't make me give it back, will she?*

17

DJ LOST EVERY VIDEO GAME.

"Don't feel bad, darlin', they beat me every time, too." Joe patted her on the head as he walked by.

When the twins asked her to play the game again, she shook her head. "Not with you two sharks. Get your uncle to play." She heaved herself to her feet. It had been at least an hour since brunch—surely there was something out there to eat. She snagged a candy-cane cookie off the silver three-tiered platter on the dining room table and meandered into the kitchen. Lindy, Gran, and Sonya sat at the kitchen table drinking coffee.

"Where's everyone else?" DJ dunked her cookie in Gran's coffee cup.

"If you mean the big, strong men, they crashed." Sonya lifted her cup in salute. "I hear the monsters mangled you out there. Don't feel bad—Shawna's the only one who can hold a candle to them. They're better with that joy stick than I'll ever be."

"But they're not even six years old yet. Scary." DJ leaned against Gran's shoulder. "Sure smells good in here."

"Is that a hint?" Gran wrapped her arm around DJ's waist.

"Could be called that. I mean, if you had something to

offer a starving child, she wouldn't turn it down." DJ tried to make her voice and face pitiful.

"Cinnamon roll?"

"Are there any left?" DJ's voice dropped to a whisper.

"Enough to last until dinner. Check the bread box."

"You make the best cinnamon rolls in the whole world." DJ set the gooey roll on a paper plate and put it in the microwave.

"You know, it's not fair—if I ate like my kid does, I'd weigh three hundred pounds," Lindy observed.

"I know how you feel." Sonya reached over and snagged a bite off the roll when DJ set her plate on the table.

"You want one? I'll fix it." DJ looked from one to the other. Sonya nodded and Lindy shook her head. "Take that one, and I'll make me another."

"You mean just because I peeled off the best part, it's mine?"

"Something like that." DJ grinned at the teasing and flinched when she heard the thunder of the twins' feet. "Quick, bar the door!"

"DJ, can we go riding now?" The twins glanced at the food set out and flung themselves at DJ's legs. "We was good forever. We beat Shawna, too."

"That makes you the champs. Go ask your grandpa. If he says 'yes,' it's okay with me."

"Me too?" Shawna leaned against her mother. "They beat me."

The boys charged out at top speed. These days, that seemed to be their only speed.

"Walk, please. No running in the house," Gran called.

The thunder turned to soft patters, but giggles floated back.

"Just think, Lindy," Sonya said after licking the caramel goo from her fingertips, "in a couple of months, you'll hear that all the time."

"I know, and it sometimes scares me to bits."

DJ looked up and watched her mother's face.

"How do you direct all that energy? I've never been around little boys—in fact, I've hardly been around small children at all. The times they've been at our house, no matter how good they've been, they're just always so busy." Lindy sneaked a bite of cinnamon roll. "Wears me out."

"You'll get used to it. It's good that Robert plans on keeping the nanny."

"Yeah, at least for a while, until I decide if I'll quit my job or not."

DJ nearly choked on the last bite.

Lindy looked over at her and smiled. "Shocker, huh?"

"Really?"

"We've been talking about it. My professor is so interested in my thesis on entrepreneurial kids that he keeps encouraging me to turn it into a book. He says I write well enough. Maybe my mother and my daughter aren't the only ones with all the talent." She looked over at Sonya. "Actually, DJ and Amy gave me the idea."

DJ rolled her eyes. "Yeah, as if all our tries to earn money worked." *What would it be like to have her mother home all the time?*

"Well, some better than others. Look at your note card sales. You cleaned out your inventory before Christmas."

"I think they're wonderful. If I'd have known you were selling them, I'd have bought enough to give to the people in my office for gifts," Sonya said.

"I'll always have more." DJ winked at her. She could feel her insides go all warm and fuzzy at the compliment. All those she'd left at the Academy sold, too. And she now had three commissions to draw member horses. Crazy, here when she finally had an actual way to make money, she already had a saddle. Now maybe her saddle fund could go for clinics and stuff. Of course, Major needed new shoes. . . .

Giving the kids rides at the Academy an hour later reminded her of the pony parties. But with Joe taking the twin who wasn't riding Bandit with him on Ranger, and Shawna on Major, DJ had much more fun. She caught the twins' giggles and passed them back.

Shawna had stars in her eyes for the rest of the day after riding Major all by herself.

The next two days flew by like the seconds in a jumping ring. Shawna would have ridden all day and night if allowed. She helped DJ saddle soap her new saddle and chattered nonstop about her dream horse.

Since it was a weekend, Robert and the boys were about. One day they all headed for Marine World Africa USA in Vallejo less than an hour away. By the time they'd seen all the shows, including two visits to the killer whale show, had a butterfly sit on Shawna's shoulder in the butterfly house, and sampled all the food items, they could barely make it back to the car. Only once did DJ wish she could have spent the sunny day riding.

"He's here," Lindy called up the stairs late Monday morning.

"I know, I'm zipping my bag." DJ took one last look around the room and slung the canvas tote over her shoulder. She had packed her boots, rain gear, everyday clothes, and, at her mother's insistence, an outfit dressier than jeans and a sweat shirt. She'd had a hard time closing the zipper. With her other hand she picked up the package wrapped in Christmas tree paper and headed down the stairs. Joe had helped her frame another of her drawings as a gift for Brad and Jackie. As Joe had said when she'd worried over whether they'd like it: if they didn't, that was their problem, not hers. Easy to say, harder to live with.

"Now, remember, if you want to come home early, all you have to do is call," Lindy whispered in DJ's ear as she gave her a good-bye hug.

"I know." *She must think I'm a baby or something.* DJ hugged her mother back. "See ya."

"I promise to return her safely," Brad said with a smile.

"I know. And thank you for the lovely basket of goodies." Lindy crossed her arms over her chest. "You have fun now. And behave yourself."

DJ rolled her eyes. "M-o-t-h-e-r."

"That's okay, I'm paid to say that." Lindy tried to smile. "Comes with being a mother."

"Thank you for letting her come with me," Brad said. "Jackie and I really appreciate it."

"You're welcome."

DJ felt like running in place. Did everyone have to be so . . . so polite? It wasn't as if she was going to the moon, for Pete's sake. "Bye, Mom." Would she get the hint?

Once in the car, Brad asked, "Would you like to show me your horse before we go?"

"Sure." DJ slammed the heel of her hand against her forehead. "Sorry, I meant to tell you thanks for the awesome saddle first thing."

"You like it then?"

"Like it? Does the sun rise every day? I couldn't believe it. And a Crosby, to boot."

"I wanted to get you a Hermes, but Jackie said no, you'd be afraid to use it."

"A Hermes?" her voice squeaked. She swallowed. "I

would have kept it under lock and key in my bedroom. What if someone stole it?"

"Then this is better. Does it fit you and Major okay?"

"Same size I already use—only so much better. I was saving for a used saddle." DJ pointed at Amy's drive. "Stop here."

By the time they'd picked up Amy, stopped to see Major, and were finally on the road, Brad asked if they were hungry. "Because if you can hold out, Jackie will have lunch ready."

"We can wait."

"Okay, then I'll just get us drinks." He swung into a fast-food place.

Talking with Brad was a lot like visiting with Robert, DJ decided by the time they reached Santa Rosa. Comfortable and easy. Of course any time she could talk horses, that made conversation easy.

He told her how he'd gotten interested in Arabians and begun breeding them back when the breed was rising in value astronomically. Jackie did most of the training and showing, but her true love was dressage. A few years later, they had bought her Hanovarian, Lord Byron.

"She's looking forward to helping you if you want," he continued. "I thought you might like to ride Matadorian. He's a real sweetheart."

"Your stallion?" DJ couldn't believe her ears.

"Sure, why not? And, Amy, there's a mare with your name on her. You do ride English, don't you?"

"Not usually, but I can. DJ made sure I learned," Amy answered.

"Amy thinks Western is best. She and Josh—he's half Arab—do really well."

When they drove into the curving, oak-lined drive, DJ couldn't take in everything quickly enough. White board fences checkerboarded the rolling pastures, where horses grazed knee-deep in grass. The stone house was set off on a rise, and the road curved on around to the type of barn she'd seen in pictures of Kentucky. On the roof two cupolas topped by horse weather vanes stood etched against the blue sky. White siding matched the fences, setting off the window and door trim painted a hunter green. A covered, open-sided arena shared one wall with an open ring that looked at least an acre in size.

"Oh, my." DJ couldn't think of anything else to say.

"I think I've died and gone to heaven," Amy whispered.

Inside the house, after greeting Jackie, DJ gravitated to the wall-to-wall and floor-to-ceiling bank of windows that looked out over the pastures backed by the rocky coastal mountain range. Rows of grapes, now barren for the winter, threaded the lower slopes. A couple of yearlings raced across their pasture, tails flagging in the Arabian way. A flock of ducks came in low over the pond at the end of the manicured lawn and slid their way onto the smooth water.

"This is one of my favorite places, too." Her father came up to stand beside her. "I never tire of watching the land change with the seasons. We'll go down after lunch and I'll introduce you to my other kids." At the question on her face, he added, "The horses, my dear. Not human relatives."

DJ shot him a grin and turned back to the scene. "Sure is beautiful out there."

"I think you and I have even more in common than I dreamed." He took her arm. "Come on, I'll show you to your room and then we'll have lunch. Amy, you want to share a room with this long drink of water or you want one of your own?"

"We'll share. I just wish I'd brought my camera. I can't believe I left it at home."

"You didn't!"

Amy nodded. "I know, you can hit me later."

"You're welcome to use one of ours. You can take your pick." Brad showed them up a curving stairway graced by framed pictures of Arabians in all stages of show and growth. It would take hours just to see them all. An oil painting of a chestnut stallion, wind whipping his mane, held the place of honor. The wide gold-leaf frame brought out the gold in his coat.

"That's Matadorian, my pride and joy, when he was three. He's heavier now that he's mature, so he looks even better. And the foals he sires—winners all." He pushed open a door and ushered them in. "Here's your room. Hope you like it." He glanced at his watch. "I have one phone call I have to return, so I'll meet you in the kitchen. Jackie said to tell you the drawers are empty if you want to put your things in them. Bathroom's through there."

DJ flopped down on the queen-sized bed. "This has enough pillows to start a store. Can you believe this place?"

"Makes you wonder, huh?" Amy flopped beside DJ.

"About what?"

"About why he never wrote to you or anything? It isn't like he couldn't afford it."

"Yeah, I thought of that. Maybe sometime I'll ask him." DJ bounded back to her feet. "Let's go eat. I want to ride Matadorian." She picked up her wrapped package and headed out the door.

When they were all sitting at the round country table surrounded by bay windows, she handed her father the gift. After seeing all the paintings and portraits around the house, she felt silly even giving it to him.

Amy handed her packet of note cards to Jackie. "To say thanks for inviting me."

"DJ, did you really draw this?" Brad held the enlarged picture of the furry-eared foal up to get more light, then handed it to Jackie. DJ nodded. "I know you said you liked to draw, but this is better than something a hobbyist would do. You're a real artist. You taken any lessons?"

"From Gran—sorta. And I'm in art class at school." DJ shrugged. "I just like to draw horses. Been doing it ever since I can remember."

"Amy, are these your photos?" Jackie had looked at the back of the unwrapped package.

Now it was Amy's turn to squirm a bit. "Uh-huh. DJ and I made packets of note cards using some of her drawings and my photos. It's our latest business."

"They're lovely." Jackie smiled across the table. "You mean there have been other businesses?"

By the time they'd all laughed at Amy and DJ's tales of business mishaps and devoured their lunch, clouds had set in.

"Let me go set this on my desk and change clothes so we can all go riding. We'll show you the rest of the farm—especially down by the river. Better hurry before the rain hits." Brad pushed back his chair. "Thank you for the drawing, DJ. You have no idea how much this means to me."

That night Amy and DJ curled up on the bed after saying good-night to Brad and Jackie. The girls plumped pillows under their chins and waved their feet in the air.

"I cannot believe that horse," DJ whispered. "Riding Matadorian was like . . . like . . ." She couldn't think of anything to compare it to.

"I know." Amy's voice held the same tone of reverence. "I could get used to living in a place like this, with plenty of awesome horses to choose from. Poor Josh would get jealous." She laid her cheek on the pillow and looked at DJ. "To think your dad let me ride his stallion, too. Go figure."

My dad—the words were becoming more familiar. DJ sighed. Tomorrow she could ride Jackie's dressage horse,

Lord Byron, if she wanted. Shame they didn't have a jumping setup, too—then the farm would have been complete. She had a feeling if she asked, the jumps would appear as if by magic.

Once home, DJ chattered nonstop about her father's horses, his farm, his trophies, his house, his wife, and what fun he was. When she finally ran down, she noticed the two creases between her mother's eyebrows now looked more like ditches.

"And he said to tell you thank you for letting me visit. He hopes we can do this more often."

"I'm sure he does. I'm glad you had such a good time. Joe said he'll be by about eight." Lindy rose from her curled position in the corner of the sofa. "I have to leave for work early in the morning, so I'm going to bed. You'll stay at Gran's tomorrow night because I'll be in Los Angeles. My number's on the message board." She stopped with one foot on the stair. "I'm glad you're home, Darla Jean, and that you had fun."

DJ looked after her. *Yeah, right—you look thrilled to bits*. What was bugging her mother now?

18

YOU KNOW YOU'RE NOT SUPPOSED to be listening. *Look what happened last time.*

The battle waged back and forth in her mind. *But if I don't listen, I won't know what's going on. Nobody ever tells me anything.*

DJ sat on the stairs. It wasn't her fault they were talking so loudly she could hear. She'd been on her way to bed when the noise stole her attention. She wrapped both arms around her knees and propped her chin on them.

"You should have heard her, babbling on about how wonderful the Atwoods are. All the things they have, the house, the horses . . . you name it, the Atwoods have it—in spades. Along with a little diamond dust."

"Lindy, she's just a kid. Sure she's impressed. We'd probably *all* be impressed. Sounds like Brad has done really well for himself."

DJ strained to hear. Her mother mumbled something.

"Oh, Lindy, darling, he isn't trying to take her away from you. You've been a good mother and—"

"No, I haven't, Robert. Gran raised DJ, not me. We might as well have been sisters for as much responsibility as I took. I went to work, to school, came home and studied. Seems I've been doing that all of my life. Then it was on to more school, traveling with the job, climbing the corporate ladder—for what?"

"Hey, take it easy on yourself. You can't tell me that your income wasn't important around here. You did the best you could. Anyone can tell this family's offered up a lot of prayers."

"That's due to Gran, too. I . . . I kind of gave up on prayer, on God, a long time ago. He didn't seem to answer any of my prayers, so I quit praying and left it up to my mother like I did everything else. How can I blame Brad for not accepting his responsibility when I didn't accept mine either?"

"Oh, Lindy, if you didn't have faith, we wouldn't be getting married."

"Well, I'm not a heathen, you know."

"That's what I said. And now our faith will grow together and our families will blend with God's blessing. It's going to work out—perhaps Brad and Jackie will just become a part of our extended family. We can make room for everyone in our lives—you can never run out of love because it just keeps growing to encompass more people. Instead of worrying about Brad taking DJ away, we can share our lovely daughter with him. We'll all be richer for it."

There was a silence long enough for DJ to think she'd heard it all, but as she started to move, her mother's voice came again. "I wish I could forbid her to see him. I just have a feeling something horrible is going to come of all this."

DJ felt her stomach clench. "Something horrible? Come on, Mom, give me a break," she whispered the words as if hearing them might remove the yucky feeling in the pit of her stomach.

"Well, since that's not possible, we'll just take this one day at a time. We'll get through it."

Robert again. At least *he* didn't think her father was a monster from outer space.

"How come you're so wise?" Lindy's voice no longer wore the edge of panic.

"I prayed for wisdom—and keep on praying for it. I think I'm going to need it even more in the months ahead, don't you?"

"Are you sure you still want to marry me?"

When they started to get mushy, DJ went to bed. *Good thing I never told her that Brad said there was always a room for me at his house if I felt I needed to leave here*. She sighed. But that wouldn't happen. Not in a million years. Even though he'd said she could bring Major.

"God, please help me to be really nice to my mother. I want us always to get along like we have lately. Thank you for such a wonderful Christmas and all the family you've given me. Amen."

Before she turned out the lights, she took out her journal and, propping herself against the head of her bed, began to write. And write. There was so much to think about, to wonder over, and to look forward to. The pages filled quickly.

"Well, that ought to impress Mrs. Adams even though I didn't write every day." She slapped the notebook closed and stuffed it back into its drawer. Maybe tomorrow she could go riding up in Briones.

A thought DJ hadn't had for a long time floated through her mind just before she fell asleep: Maybe they would all have an easier time if she weren't there to mix things up. She turned over. Well, if she ever needed a place to run to, she had one now.

DJ's first wish in the morning was to fire the weather

reporters. Instead of clear sky as they'd promised, heavy rain washed her windows again. She pulled the covers over her head and tried to go back to sleep, flipping first one way, then the other. The wind and rain sounded as though they were coming right into the house.

She flopped around again. A ringing sound floated down the hall. "The phone?" She bailed out of bed and dashed to her mother's bedroom, home to the closest phone. "Hello?"

"DJ?"

"Who'd you think?" She sank down onto the already-made bed, her gaze traveling around the room. You'd think no one lived in her mother's room, it was always so disgustingly neat.

"Come on, darlin', you can wake up more chipper than that."

"I was already awake, Joe, but it's pouring out."

"That's why I'm planning to give you a ride. You suppose Amy wants a ride, too?"

When everything was set for their trip to do morning chores, DJ hung up the phone and got busy. Joe had said he'd be there in fifteen minutes, and he was never late. Food bars for breakfast again. She should have stayed up when she first awoke. Grumbling at herself, she dressed and headed down the stairs. No time to straighten her room now.

All the early riders at the Academy were as sick of rain as DJ. A couple complained of leaks above their stalls, and the outside stalls had water running through them. Several maintenance men were digging trenches on the hill above the stalls to divert the runoff.

DJ looked longingly up at the hills she knew lurked behind the sheeting rain. "Major, I want to ride up there again s-o-o bad, don't you?" He obligingly nuzzled her shoulder and whuffled in her ear. "Hey, that tickles!" DJ scratched the crisp hairs on his upper lip and made him twitch, then nibble at her fingers. When he licked her palm, she threw her arms around his neck. "You are the best horse in the whole world."

"Then get him out into the arena and make him earn his keep." Joe was grooming Ranger in the neighboring stall.

"Sheesh, what a slave driver. Don't you know I'm on vacation?" She picked up her brushes and went to work on Major's thick winter coat. "How come you get so dirty just standing in a stall? What would you be like if you were on pasture?"

"He will be soon, if Robert has his way. That house of his is shaping up fast. He's already got the fences repaired and a new roof on the barn." Joe raised his voice. "Hey, Amy, you sleeping out there?"

"In this weather? Give me a break! I've got to work fast—we're going to visit my other grandparents this weekend. I thought we were going tomorrow but—"

"So you won't be here to go up in Briones with me?"

"DJ, have you looked outside lately?"

"It's going to stop—I know it will. You can go with me, can't you, Joe?"

"Nope. Since it's raining, Mel and I are going into the city to the new art museum and then to the opera."

"Opera?" DJ made the word sound disgusting.

"That's exactly why we didn't invite you, though Gran said you could do with some artistic training."

"In opera?"

"Don't act like it would kill you. You can thank me for saving you from that fate worse than death."

"Thanks, Joe. I'll feed Ranger for you." DJ retrieved her

saddle from the half-door and set it atop the pad. How she would love to be using her new saddle, but she wasn't about to let it get rained on . . . yet. "Guess I'll just give Patches an extra-long workout and catch up on some tack cleaning."

"Not if you want a ride home." Joe led Ranger out of his stall and swung aboard. "I'm leaving at eleven."

Later DJ wandered around the house, feeling as if her last friend had deserted her. The place felt clammy, so she started a fire in the fireplace, turned on the Christmas tree lights and music, and, after fixing herself a ham and cheese sandwich, brought her sketch pad down to go to work. Now was as good a time as any to get started on those three commissions.

Sometime later, she looked up and let out a whoop of joy. Sunshine—watery for sure, but real sunshine—beamed in the windows. She ran to the French doors and studied the sky. Even the Western sky shone blue instead of the all-too-usual gray or black.

She dashed off a quick note to her mother, *Gone riding in Briones*, grabbed her rain gear, just in case, and pelted out the door. Her rear wheel threw up enough water to soak an elephant on the speed-breaking ride, making DJ glad she'd put on the slicker. She tacked Major up with the same lightning speed and trotted up the trail before anyone could find something else that needed her attention.

It took great force of will to ignore the nagging voice that reminded her it was always wiser to ride with a buddy. In fact, buddy trail riding was rule of the Academy. *It's not my fault all my buddies are gone. I'm not about to waste the sunshine*.

The washed-out stretch on the fire road flowed deeper

and wider, but Major splashed right through it. Birds twittered and chirped in the trees overhead, and high above the hill she could see a pair of turkey vultures catching the thermals on broad wings. Cows bellowed for their offspring, and the creek played bass in crescendo power. DJ hummed along, the words running through her mind: *And Mary's boy child, Jesus Christ, was born on Christmas Day.* She liked the song's catchy Latino rhythm.

When they crested the hill to the meadow, she groaned. Clouds were sneaking peeks over the tops of the Western hills. "Too bad, you can just hold off. We're taking a new trail today, and a little more rain won't stop us."

Major snorted as if he agreed. When she turned off before climbing to the bluebird saddle and angled along the side of the hill on what looked more like a cow path than a trail, he trotted willingly along. Ears flicking back and forth, he kept track of all the sounds around them.

DJ left off the humming and started singing. She sure wasn't an opera star, but with no one to hear her and make faces if she wasn't exactly on key, she felt free to really sing. From here, DJ could see more of the straits. She stopped once to watch an oil tanker make its way upstream, and the breeze kicked in. It was beginning to feel a little wild.

They came around a corner and Major stopped. Some of the hill had slipped and covered the path.

"We should go back, huh, buddy?"

Major's ears flicked. He lowered his head to sniff the trail.

"But look, it's only a few feet. We'll go down and around." She turned Major off the track, and watching for ground squirrel holes, they made their way back up to the track. DJ stood in her stirrups. They should meet up with one of the main trails again pretty soon. They'd take that one back.

The clouds seemed to be racing to the east. While the

sun was putting up a battle royal, it was definitely losing.

They rounded another curve, and the hillside below dropped off.

Major stopped. DJ nudged him forward.

"Come on, fella, what's the deal?" She squeezed her knees again. He quivered.

Major took two more tentative steps forward—and the hill dissolved around them. Panicked, DJ slammed her legs into his sides. Major leaped forward, but the moving mud carried him with it.

Too scared to scream, DJ kept a firm hand on the reins to help hold her horse upright. He leaped again, trying to slog their way out. A young oak tree quivered on the lip of the cliff.

DJ grabbed for it. Rough bark bit into her hands.

She clung and felt the saddle slip out from under her. Quickly, she kicked her feet free of the stirrups. There was nothing more she could do.

Major screamed as he slid over the edge of the cliff.

19

"MAJOR!"

All DJ heard in response was the ominous rumble of sliding, saturated clay.

"God, please help me." She kicked against the face of the cliff, searching for a toehold—anything. Her arms felt like they were being pulled right out of the sockets. She tried to look down, but that put more pressure on her shoulders. She looked up instead. The lip of the cliff wasn't so far away. If only she could get a toehold. . . .

She dug into the hard clay with the toe of her boot. Finally she came into contact with a round, solid piece. Sandstone. Praying, whimpering, the pain growing more unbearable, she dug with her foot around the top of the stone.

Keep a cool head. She could hear Bridget's voice in her ear. "I can do all things. I can do all things." She sobbed out the verse. "God, please help."

How far down was the bottom? How was Major? *Get a toehold!* With one more kick, she could feel enough solid foundation under her foot to stand—with the toe of one boot. The relief from even that small help brought tears to DJ's eyes. She took in a deep breath. "Thank you."

Kicking with the other foot created enough space for

her to balance on. She let go of the oak with one hand and looked down. The cliff fell away beneath her to a ledge, then fell away again. She could see no farther.

"Major!" She tried to whistle, but her lips couldn't manage it. Besides, you had to have spit to whistle.

The clouds rolled over the hill like a puffy gray waterfall, sending tendrils down to drip in her face.

Her right foot cramped, sending pain shooting up her leg. She shifted the weight to the left and clamped harder on the tree. Stretching her right leg, she tried to release the cramp but failed.

How to escape her trap? Could she go down? Sideways? Mountain climbing had never been one of her aspirations, but she'd watched rock-climbing on TV. How did they do it?

She reached out with her right hand, searching for anything to grab on to. A chunk of dirt broke away. DJ's heart leaped back into her throat, racing as if to burst out of her chest. Back to the oak. She sighed in relief as she grasped it with her left hand. The cramp let up. If only she hadn't tied her slicker on behind her saddle—so what if it hadn't been raining.

"Major!"

Was that a nicker she heard? She called again. Only a crow answered, his harsh caw anything but comforting.

No one knows where I am. The thought sent her heart into overdrive again. "Come on, DJ, keep a cool head." Talking out loud helped. "Okay, now start with the left hand." She looked to the left, imagining this hand move over the surface of the cliff.

Giving up on her hands for the moment, she began kicking a broader shelf for her feet to rest on. She focused all her concentration on her feet. The slippery wet clay clung to her boot, threatening to make her lose her balance, but DJ kept on kicking.

The wind blowing up the river cut through her sweat shirt as though it wasn't even there. She shivered and kept on kicking until she could finally stand on both feet. DJ breathed a sigh of relief. Her legs shook. Her arms ached. She shivered again, this time more like a shudder.

The mist grew heavier, turning to rain. The sky darkened and wind whipped the trees.

"Help!" she screamed as loud as she could. What other idiot would be out in the park late on a day like today? DJ screamed again. And again. Until her throat closed in pain.

Who would look for her? Her mother wouldn't be home from work yet, and Gran and Joe weren't coming home till late. No one knew where she was. Tears joined the raindrops sliding down her cheeks.

I know where you are. DJ sucked in a breath. Of course—God knew where she was. "Then how about telling someone else? Please, please, make someone come And please, please let Major be okay. Please keep him from suffering, God." The thought of her horse in pain made the tears flow again. "Please."

Should she just let go? How far down was down? What was below her? She tried to figure out the landscape, but this was new territory.

"Bridget'll kill me for letting myself get caught in a situation like this after all the years she's drummed safety in our heads." Talking out loud helped drive the darkness back. "Okay, God, what do I do?"

The smell of wet clay filled her nostrils as she hugged the cliff. What a way to spend an evening.

As soon as she stopped talking, panic stalked her. Panic that made her stomach roil, like it would leap out of her throat. Panic that set her heart to pounding and made her weak knees even weaker.

"So sing." She forced the words past the huge lump in her throat. "The Lord liveth, and blessed be the rock . . ."

That one came easily since she was sort of standing on a rock, more grateful for a piece of solid earth than she'd ever dreamed possible. She continued the verse and found another song, then another—each like a friend come to comfort her. DJ set her verse to music. "I can do all things, I can do all things . . ." The tears streaming down her face made singing hard. "I can do all things through Christ who strengthens me."

When she could no longer force the words and tune past her parched throat, she sang them in her mind.

Huddled by herself on the face of a cliff in the dark and pouring rain, DJ could sense that she wasn't alone. Not really. How much time had passed? How long since darkness fell? She had no idea.

What was that? A horse whinny? "Major." What she thought would be a yell barely went farther than the face of the cliff.

"DJ!" A voice came from far away, then a whinny again—this time from the same direction as the voice. And then an answering one from below her.

Major was alive!

"D-e-e-e J-a-a-ay!" The voice sounded closer.

"I'm here." She gathered all her strength and tried again. "Here, over here! Thank you, God. Thank you, Jesus. Oh, thank you!"

A light pierced the darkness coming around the side of the hill. Whoever it was must be on the trail she took earlier.

"DJ!" The shout again.

Another whinny from someplace below her.

"Keep at it, horse, you can make more noise than I can. Please, God, give me strength to holler." She sniffed and wriggled her dripping nose. "I'm here. Down here!"

The light stopped above them. "DJ?"

"Joe! I'm down here . . . on the cliff."

"Easy, kid, I'm coming for you." Never had a voice sounded more like love in action.

A chunk of dirt broke away and went crashing past her. "Stay back—the bank will give again." More dirt and clumps of grass cascaded by her left shoulder. The oak tree trembled. "Stay back!"

"Can you hang on, darlin'?" His voice came from farther away this time.

"I'm okay—now. Major is down below me somewhere. He heard you first and whinnied."

"I know, that's what brought us here. Are you hurt?"

"No."

"Thank you, God! Okay."

She heard the crackle of a radio and someone else giving instructions.

"DJ, we've got a rope here that we can send over the side. Can you get the loop over your head and down under your arms, or do you need one of us to help you?"

"I can do it. I've got a little piece of rock cleared to stand on."

"Okay, here it comes."

She could hear movements overhead and another voice or two. She watched the glare of the lights, and slowly a looped rope came into view.

DJ reached with her left arm and tried to snag it. "More to the right." The rope swung closer. DJ grabbed the loop and slipped her left arm into it. Then, depending on the rope for support, she let go with her right and pulled the loop over her head. "Ready."

"Okay, now, if you can lean back in the rope and walk up the cliff, it will be easier on your arms. Think you can do that? Just brace your feet against the cliff and walk up it."

DJ gripped the rope with both hands, and with the loop holding her secure, she did exactly as Joe instructed. She walked up the cliff and right into his arms. The men with him cheered.

"Oh, DJ, I . . . thank you, Lord." He held her closer and rubbed her back. "You're soaked and frozen clear through."

One of the men handed her his jacket. "Here, put this on."

DJ slid her aching arms into the sleeves. "Joe, how'd you get here? I thought you went to the opera with Gran?"

"Something told me to go home." He zipped the jacket for her since her fingers couldn't. "I'll never question God's prompting again."

"How'd you find me?"

"Ma'am," replied one of the other men, his Southern drawl obviously put on, "I learned trackin' back in the Boy Scouts. We just followed yo tra-il."

"In the dark?" DJ's voice squeaked past her sore throat.

"Let's get her out of here," another ordered.

"What about Major? I can't leave without Major."

"Here, put this around you." Another man held out a heat-trapping emergency blanket. "This will trap your body heat and warm you even more."

"Joe, I can't go yet. What about Major?" DJ grabbed the front of his jacket. "I won't leave him." She stared up at his shadowed face, the light catching the raindrops on his slicker.

"Joe, ETA for the chopper is five minutes."

"No!" DJ clutched the blanket around her. "I can't leave Major."

"DJ, listen to me. I will go down there and check on him."

"No, let me, Cap'n. I've got fewer years on my carcass," one of the younger officers said with a grin. "Besides, we do these all the time—you've been out to pasture."

Joe snorted, but keeping one arm wrapped tightly

around DJ as if she might run away from him, he agreed.

The younger officer wrapped the rope around his waist and between his legs, then gave the thumbs-up signal.

"Belay on," someone called from above—and over the cliff he went.

DJ shuddered at the thought of Major down in the darkness over the edge. The warmth of the blanket and Joe's arm around her helped to keep her steady. "I know he's alive, Joe."

"He's a tough old horse—wise too."

"But what if he's hurt . . . bad?" She stumbled over the words.

"That could be. But since these hills are all clay with so few rocks and trees, that old horse has a good chance. We'll just have to have faith that God is in control. He will lead us through whatever is ahead." Joe hugged her again. "He led us to you, didn't He?"

The walkie-talkie crackled in his hand.

"Joe here."

"Yeah, Captain, we got a problem down here. This horse is stuck in the mud halfway up his rib cage."

"See any injuries?"

"Only dirt and more dirt, but I can't see his legs."

"How's his breathing?"

"Seems to be okay. He looks alert, just stuck."

"Come on up. We'll talk about what to do."

DJ could hear the *thwunk, thwunk* of an incoming helicopter.

"Over and out."

"Cap'n, that chopper can't put down here, so I'm having him land in the meadow. We can all ride out there to meet it. You want her to go home on it, right?"

"Right."

"No! Joe, I'm staying with Major." DJ flung herself at Joe's chest. "Please, Joe, *please*." She could feel herself spinning out of control. "I can't leave him!"

"No, you aren't staying, child. That hill could give way again."

"But then Major . . ." The horror of what could happen to her horse was too terrible for DJ to contemplate.

20

"LET ME GO DOWN THERE TO SEE HIM, JOE. Please!"

"No, darlin', I can't."

Fury, burning, raging fury, made DJ shake. She bit her lip till she could taste blood. "He's my horse." With every ounce of control keeping her from plunging back down the hill to Major, she whispered it again. "Major is my horse."

"And you're my granddaughter." As Joe swung aboard Ranger, DJ darted to the lip of the hill. An officer grabbed her around the middle and carried her kicking back to Ranger. With a shake of his head, Joe offered her a hand to swing up behind him. "DJ, I've been a policeman all my life, and I will *always* put a human life ahead of an animal's. Even more so when I love that stubborn girl as much as life itself."

DJ settled herself behind him and looked over her shoulder to see the younger officer that had gone down to check on Major standing with the others.

"Don't worry, DJ," the younger man called. "We'll get him out in the morning when we can see to dig. He's okay for the night."

Unless the hill slides down over him. She forced herself to call back, "Thank you."

"DJ, I know you are absolutely furious with me, but that's the way it is. Melanie is waiting at the staging parking lot. The rescue team might decide to take you in to the hospital for observation."

I don't think so, DJ argued back inside her head. She refused to answer Joe. Somehow she had to get back up to Major.

They bundled her aboard the helicopter and wrapped her in more blankets. While she'd felt the warmth of the one, she still shook from the cold. Someone else handed her a mug of hot, sugared coffee.

"Sorry, we didn't bring hot chocolate. Can you drink this?"

DJ nodded, but her teeth clanked on the cup rim when she put it to her mouth.

A television station van was set up in the parking lot—she could see it as they came in for a landing. Her mom and Robert were there, too.

DJ felt the tears burn behind her eyes. *Don't you dare cry,* she ordered herself. But that was easier said than done. When Gran, her mom, and Robert wrapped their arms around her, she couldn't live up to her orders.

"Major is stuck in the mud, and it's all my fault." Deep, tearing sobs ripped through her. "If he dies, it's all my fault."

"How about if we check her over?" a young female emergency medical technician asked.

"I'm not going in any ambulance, and I'm *not* going to a hospital."

"Darla Jean," her mother said firmly, "you will do what is needed."

"Can we ask you a couple of questions?" A tape recorder appeared in front of DJ's face as if by magic. A reporter held the other end.

"How about I answer questions while the medical personnel attend to her." Robert turned DJ over to the medical crew with one arm, and the reporter away with the other.

The young woman sat DJ down on the rear edge of the ambulance and popped a thermometer in her mouth and a blood pressure cuff on her arm.

"I'm fine—just cold." Talking with the thermometer in her mouth wasn't easy, but DJ managed.

"Sure you are, kid. You want us to be out of a job? If we don't check you out, my boss'll yell at me. You don't want that to happen, do you?"

DJ glared at her.

Once the plastic thing was out of her mouth, DJ took in a deep breath. "Look, I'm not hurt. I ache all over, but what do you expect?"

"Your temp is subnormal, but not down to dangerous hypothermia levels. Pulse is fine, too. I guess you can go."

"I told you so."

"I know you did. Let's just hope and pray your horse comes out in as good a condition as you."

"Thanks." DJ ran her tongue over her chewed lip. "Sorry I was a brat."

"Don't blame you a bit. Take care now."

The ambulance and the TV van left at the same time. DJ climbed into Robert's car with Gran on one side of her and Lindy on the other—they acted as if she needed guarding or something. Could they read her mind, trying a million ways of going back for Major?

Later after a long soak in the bathtub, and wearing sweats and her heavy bathrobe, DJ returned to the family room.

"How you doing, darlin'?" Gran brought a tray from the kitchen. She handed DJ the steaming mug of hot chocolate and offered coffee to the others.

"I'm fine, thanks."

"I put a bit of coffee in that."

DJ knew Gran was trying make things right for her. Leave it to Gran, she could still read her granddaughter like a book. "Where's Joe?"

Silence fell. The adults exchanged looks.

"Is Major all right?" Panic clawed at her middle again.

"DJ, Joe is camping right by Major. He said to tell you that you can go up there first thing in the morning."

"He can but I couldn't."

"Well, he has a few more supplies than you did," Lindy noted, the furrows obvious between her eyes. "And people there to help him if he needs it."

"Face it, DJ—he couldn't leave his old buddy up there alone any more than you could." Robert raised his coffee mug in a salute. "That's my dad."

They started digging as soon as it was light, Joe told her later. It took four men two hours to dig around Major enough to slide a sling under his belly. DJ arrived when they were digging his legs free so the helicopter could airlift him out.

"Hey, big guy." She threw her arms around his neck, kneeling in the mud in front of him. Major whuffled and nosed her pockets. "You knew I'd bring you something, didn't you?" She looked over at Joe, who looked like he'd been sunk in the mud himself.

"He's okay, darlin'." His nod gave her as much assurance as his words.

"Th-thanks." She opened a canteen she brought and gave Major a drink, then rationed the horse cookies she'd stuffed in her pockets. Another couple of hours passed, the sloppy mud slowing the digging. All through it, Major never floundered around or fought their efforts. He stood perfectly still, only quivering at times.

Joe finally ordered the helicopter to return. It hovered above them, the rotors drowning any talking. A hook descended on a cable, and the men worked together to hook it to the sling.

DJ kept up a running monologue in Major's ear, stroking his neck and face to keep him calm.

"Okay!" Joe yelled, at the same time giving a signal to the man in the chopper door. "Tighten her up."

"Oh, God, please make this work." DJ held her breath as the sling tightened around Major's belly. With a gigantic sucking, the horse's legs came free, and he swung into the air. DJ dropped to the ground to keep from being hit by Major's dripping, muddy legs as the chopper lifted the horse higher and higher. Major whinnied, but even then remained still, as if he understood the importance of not flailing around.

"That's some horse," Joe said, dropping a mud-caked arm over DJ's shoulders.

"He's some horse." Brad Atwood stood by DJ as the helicopter gently set Major down in the parking lot at the Academy.

"Yeah, he is. Thanks for helping pay for the helicopter and all."

"My pleasure. I couldn't believe it when I heard your name on the news. You and that horse of yours are having your moments of fame."

"I never thought much about the reporter there last night, but wow, they filmed the airlift and everything." DJ stepped forward and took the lead shank from Joe, who'd helped hold Major while the crew unbuckled the sling. "Good fella." She wrapped her arms around Major's neck in spite of the caked-on mud. He nuzzled her pocket. "Bet you're still starved. Thirsty, too, huh? That little sip you had was a long time ago." He nudged her again till she handed him a whole horse cookie. She turned to see the television camera aimed right at them.

"You got anything you'd like to say?" the person filming asked.

"Yeah, thank you, God, for saving my miracle horse. And thanks to all those who worked so hard to get him loose, especially my grandpa Joe who spent the night in the mud with our horse."

The man gave a thumbs-up sign and clicked off the camera.

DJ ran her hands down Major's legs, checking for any strain. One front leg and one back leg felt hot. "Let's get you fed and then washed down so we can doctor you, okay?"

Major nudged her and blew gently in her hair. He rubbed his forehead on her chest and nuzzled her pocket again.

Munching on the last cookie, he followed DJ through the barn and up to his stall.

"I put warm water in for him," Tony said. "And there's molasses in his grain. My grandpa always said molasses gives extra energy."

"Thanks. He'll like that."

"I'll help you wash him. I've never seen such a muddy horse in my life."

"I can't believe you're both okay." Hilary stopped at the bars. "Over a fifty-foot cliff and still walking. Not even a real limp. He must be made of steel."

"They both are," Tony said.

Major drained one bucket, and Tony took it to refill.

DJ looked after him and then at Hilary, both of them raising an eyebrow.

"He's been real nice since—"

"Since he sprained his ankle that day. Never would have believed it if I didn't see it with my own eyes." DJ took a rubber currycomb out of the bucket, and Hilary another. They set to work combing the worst of the mud off.

Much later with Major wearing ice boots on both hot legs, DJ allowed Joe to take her home to Gran's. Brad and Jackie were still there—she could tell by their car in the drive. Robert's car was there also.

"Life sure can change fast, can't it?" She looked over to Joe as he turned the key and pulled it out of the ignition.

"Yeah, sometimes things happen out of the blue. All you can do is get through."

"Joe, I felt Jesus with me up on that cliff."

"I know He's the one who set a bug in my ear to skip the opera. I just knew we had to get home." He shook his head. "Any other woman would have made a fuss, but not your grandmother. She just said, 'Can't you drive faster, darlin'?' And to a retired policeman—can you beat that?"

"Well, I'm sure glad you were listening." DJ glanced up to see the twins come barreling out the door. "Uh-oh, better go."

They each glommed on to a leg. "DJ, we was missing you! You okay? Is Major okay?"

"He'll be okay in a couple of days, and you can see I'm fine." She bent over and hugged each of them. "Now, hang on."

She groaned as she lifted each loaded foot.

"DJ, you gonna be our sister for real?"

"Soon, guys, soon."

A wedding coming up. Not out of the blue, but another big change nonetheless. DJ stopped her straddle walk and grinned.

"Race you to the door!"

Storm Clouds

A month remains before her mother's wedding, and DJ's afraid she won't make it. Everyone's upset about something. An invitation to spend a weekend at her father's deluxe horse ranch seems to be the perfect escape. But her mother isn't pleased with DJ's growing relationship with her father. Can DJ smooth things over in time? Don't miss Book #5 in the HIGH HURDLES series!

Early Teen Fiction Series From Bethany House Publishers

(Ages 11–14)

BETWEEN TWO FLAGS • by Lee Roddy
Join Gideon, Emily, and Nat as they face the struggles of growing up during the Civil War.

THE ALLISON CHRONICLES • by Melody Carlson
Follow along as Allison O'Brian, the daughter of a famous 1940s movie star, searches for the truth about her past and the love of a family.

HIGH HURDLES • by Lauraine Snelling
Show jumper DJ Randall strives to defy the odds and achieve her dream of winning Olympic Gold.

SUMMERHILL SECRETS • by Beverly Lewis
Fun-loving Merry Hanson encounters mystery and excitement in Pennsylvania's Amish country.

THE TIME NAVIGATORS • by Gilbert Morris
Travel back in time with Danny and Dixie as they explore unforgettable moments in history.